WILD SPIRIT

MARI CARR

PRAISE FOR WILD SPIRIT

"Wild Spirit is a sweet romance with **plenty of heat**." ★★★★★ *Fedora, Goodreads*

"While it was plenty romantic (and **extremely HOT!)** there were also plenty of laughs, and (as always) the antics of the Collins never disappoint!" ★★★★★ *Jennifer with Romance the Dispatcher Book Review, Goodreads*

"I just **can't get enough** of the Collins family!" ★★★★★ *Moran, Goodreads*

"Mari Carr has a way of writing so that you are engrossed **in all of the feels**." ★★★★★ *A, Goodreads*

"Great **writing**, great **chemistry**, and a **great love story**." ★★★★★ *Jenna, Goodreads*

"Mari Carr **blows me out if the water** with everything she writes." ★★★★★ *Janet Rodman, Goodreads*

"Yvonne and Leo were a **breath of fresh air**!" ★★★★★ *Dar, Goodreads*

"Leo and Yvonne were a **fantastic couple**." ★★★★★ *Staci, Goodreads*

"I just love the Collins family, and **can't wait for the next books**!!!" ★★★★★ *Xantippi Leska, Goodreads*

"Another **great read** in the Wild Irish world." ★★★★ *Meghann Russell, Goodreads*

WILD SPIRIT

Maybe if things were different, Leo could date the woman he's suddenly longing for, the free-spirited Yvonne Collins. For her, life is an adventure; for him, life is all about work and keeping things simple so he can focus on his son.

When a tragic event upends Leo's orderly existence, he's forced to admit he can't do it all, and he can't do it alone. Yvonne feels like exactly what Leo doesn't need, until she shows him chaos isn't always bad, and letting go isn't the same thing as losing control.

PROLOGUE

"Well now, lass. What are you doing up here by yourself?" Patrick Collins had watched his granddaughter Yvonne break away from her parents, Ewan and Natalie, who were eating dinner down at the pub and escape to his old apartment above. He followed her, concerned.

"Nothing."

He had to hand it to her. At fourteen years old, she had perfected the teenage sulk. Her tone of voice and expression made it perfectly clear that she was stewing over something.

Patrick sat down next to her on the couch. "You wouldn't lie to your old Pop Pop now, would you? Come on, my dearest heart, what's got you feeling so low?"

Yvonne sighed loudly, dramatically, and Patrick fought to hide his amusement as she said, "Next weekend is the Homecoming dance at school."

Ah. He hadn't expected to get his answer so quickly. Typically, Yvonne liked to draw out her theatrics. "And am I to assume no one has asked you?"

Yvonne shot him an impatient look that told him he'd missed by a mile. "I've been asked. By three boys."

"I see. So your problem lies in that you have too many

options and you're struggling to decide who to go with. That doesn't sound like such a bad thing."

Yvonne shook her head, exasperated. Patrick loved his grandchildren—adored them actually—but he'd always found it much easier to talk to them when they were younger. The moment each of them hit twelve and hormones kicked in, he found himself adrift.

His late wife, Sunday, had always been much better with their children as they'd advanced from youngsters to tweens. After she passed, it was the older siblings who helped him navigate the tricky waters with their younger brothers and sisters.

No doubt Sunday would have been able to deduce whatever was upsetting Yvonne by now.

He, on the other hand, was completely lost. "I give up," he said, prompting the briefest grin from the young girl.

"Leo Watson didn't ask me."

Patrick considered that. "Leo? Isn't he the young man who just recently started attending your school, whose father delivers vegetables to Sunday's Side each week? And he's been here a time or two hanging out with Lochlan and Colm, yes?"

Leo's parents had homeschooled him until this year, along with his older brother and sister.

She nodded, clearly pleased he'd recalled who Leo was. "He's the hottest boy in the whole sophomore class. And the coolest. And the funniest. And—"

"I think I get the picture. So you were hoping Leo would ask you?"

"Yeah. But he doesn't even know I exist. He invited Denise Flynn instead." Yvonne rolled her eyes as if the mere thought of that was too preposterous to believe.

"Who is Denise Flynn?" he asked.

"She's a cheerleader, and she thinks her shi—" Yvonne stopped mid-curse when Patrick narrowed his eyes. His young granddaughter shared Riley's love of cooking, spending countless hours in the kitchen of the pub with her aunt. Along the way, she'd picked up more from Riley than a knack for whipping up delicious meals.

"Language," he murmured, something he'd said to Riley pretty much ever since the girl learned to talk. Not that his daughter had ever managed to curb her tendency to cuss like a sailor.

"Sorry. Denise thinks her poop doesn't stink."

Patrick resisted the urge to chuckle. The expression admittedly lacked something with the cleaner translation.

"I see," he said.

"She's super popular and nowhere near nice enough for Leo. I don't know what he sees in her when there are lots of other girls in the school who would be better for him to date. Girls who see how cool he is. Denise just said yes so she could rub it in everyone else's faces. Not because she likes him."

It appeared this young Leo still possessed that new-car smell and was benefiting from being the mysterious—and therefore, instantly fascinating—boy in a school where most of the students had known each other since kindergarten.

"And you thought Leo would ask you?"

Yvonne didn't reply immediately. An answer in itself.

"So no?"

She grimaced. "I just don't understand what he sees in her. What's wrong with me, Pop Pop?"

The tears welling in her eyes were his undoing. "Ah, lass. Now don't go feeling bad about yourself. His asking this other girl could be based on a thousand different reasons."

"Like what?" she asked, not bothering to stem the tears streaming down her freckled cheeks.

Patrick reached over and wrapped his arm around her shoulders. He was a strong man and there was very little he couldn't handle. The exception to that rule, his undoing, was and always would be his grandchildren's tears.

"Well," he said, trying to come up with any reason why a fifteen-year-old boy might overlook a lovely lass such as Yvonne.

"Maybe he only likes girls in his own grade. You're a year younger than the boy."

"So?"

So…that didn't work. "Maybe he's abiding by that—what do they call it—bro code?"

Yvonne's eyebrows shot up, and this time her smile wasn't brief or small. She laughed loudly. "Bro code, Pop Pop?"

"Leo has become good friends with your cousins, hanging out with Lochlan, Colm and Padraig quite a bit. Do you think perhaps he isn't asking you to the dance out of respect for their friendship?"

She seemed to consider that for a few minutes, then dismissed it. "No. It's not that. Paddy, Lochlan and Colm don't know I like him, so I'm sure they never warned him to stay away. And if they *did* know, I'd kick their ass—"

Patrick cleared his throat.

"Butts," she quickly amended, "if they warned him away."

Patrick tried to come up with another reason that wouldn't hurt her feelings. In truth, he couldn't imagine why any boy wouldn't want to take his pretty granddaughter to a dance. Yvonne was lovely and sweet with a bubbly personality. Of course, she did mention the other girl was a cheerleader, and as long as there were girls in short skirts shaking pom-poms, there would be an abundance of young boys hovering nearby, drooling.

Finally, he sighed. "Can I just say that fifteen-year-old boys aren't known for being very bright? I have no idea why he invited Denise to the dance over you, other than Leo is an outright fool."

Yvonne laughed and hugged him. "Oh, Pop Pop. I love you. And I think you're absolutely right. He *is* an idiot."

He thought for a moment that solved the problem, but she sobered up too quickly. "I just…it hurts. I really like him."

"I know, lass. There's nothing worse than love's cruel sting. You know, your grandma Sunday chose to go to a dance with another fella over me once when we'd just started courting. And it hurt me more than I can say."

"Grandma Sunday turned you down for a date?"

Yvonne's shocked tone amused him. While he and his beloved Sunday had had an idyllic life together, it was hard for their offspring—their children and now grandchildren—to ever conceive of a time when they weren't a couple, but were instead two young people with more pride than sense and no idea how to express their feelings.

"She did. She accepted an invitation from Conall Brannagh."

Yvonne crinkled her nose. "That's a silly name. Who was he?"

"A rich, handsome man who had a very high opinion of himself and who strutted around Killarney like he was God's gift to this planet."

"Sounds like Denise," Yvonne muttered. "So what happened with Conall?"

Patrick tried to decide how to proceed. He didn't want his confident granddaughter to feel as though she couldn't succeed in whatever she tried, that she couldn't get anything she set her mind to, but these teenage years were tricky. High school was the time to learn the hard lessons because the truth was, life wasn't always fair.

Did he encourage her to go for it, to tell this young Leo how she felt, or did he suggest that she take the safer course, the one that would save her heartache?

He sighed. These were the times when he wished Sunday was still alive. She would know the right answer, would know how to counsel their heartbroken young girl.

"Are you and Leo friends?" he asked, deciding perhaps his advice would come more easily with background information.

"Oh yeah," she said. "We hang out a lot at school. We sit at the same lunch table in the cafeteria. Him, me, Lochlan and a bunch of our other friends. We have a lot of fun."

Patrick nodded slowly. "And has he ever given you any indication that he likes you as something more than just a friend?"

Yvonne took more time answering this question. When she did, he knew she was offering him the truth. "No. He treats me like he does Lochlan. Like a buddy. Another one of the guys."

He was quiet for a moment, then he captured her gaze. "Let me ask you this, Vonnie," he said, adopting the nickname her parents used for her. "What do you think is more valuable in life —friendship or love?"

She frowned, thinking hard. "They're both important."

He nodded and reached for her hand. "Exactly. There is happiness to be found in both. Love is important, don't get me wrong, it's one of the most amazing things in life. But...friendship is just as powerful. You're young, my dear. The truth is, most of us don't find love until we're older than you are now. Because you're still growing, figuring out who you are and what you're meant to do and be in this life. This is the time to make friends, to cultivate them, to put all your energy in them. Through friendship, we learn how to interact, how to cherish someone, how to care."

"You're only fourteen, and while you may think that means you're an adult, take it from this old man who has lived a thousand lifetimes, you are but a wee kitten. Spend your high school years learning how to be a friend. Once you've accomplished that, love will come easy at a time when you're ready to embrace it."

Yvonne leaned back against the couch, her shoulders slumping. From the pensive look on her face, he knew his words had struck a chord, that she had truly listened.

"Okay," she said at last.

"That's my graceful girl, my gift."

Yvonne snorted. "Pop Pop, you've been saying that since I was born. I'm not very graceful. I'm kind of a klutz."

"That's not what those nicknames are referring to. Your name, Yvonne, means God's grace, God's gift, and that is exactly what you are. You were a gift to your parents, to this family, to me."

"I was named after my mom's sister, not because of what the name means."

Patrick grinned. "You were named after the sister your mother loved and adored above all others. The fact she gave you that name should show you exactly how much you mean to her, how much you are loved."

"I know Mom loved my aunt Yvonne. I've seen pictures and heard all the stories about her."

Yvonne's mother, Natalie, had married Patrick's son, Ewan. Patrick knew their road to happiness had been difficult because Natalie struggled with depression. A depression that had been brought on by the untimely death of her sister, Yvonne, due to a car crash when she'd only been twenty-three years old. Patrick had often felt a kinship with Natalie, the two of them engaging in quite a few conversations over the years about mourning the loss of someone close to them.

Sunday had also died young, only in her fifties when cancer claimed her. Patrick felt as though a lifetime had passed since then, his life divided in half. He'd had the Sunday years and then the years since her death.

"There is no greater tribute, no greater testament to love, than to give someone who is your everything such a meaningful name," he said. "You are a gift, Yvonne. Never forget that. If Leo isn't meant to be your love, then accept his friendship, cultivate it, and hold on to it tight. If he's as special as you say, then I suspect the two of you will be there for each other long after high school ends."

Yvonne frowned, swiping at her wet cheeks, though the tears had stopped falling. "I guess so."

She didn't sound convinced, so he made another effort.

"Let me ask you this," Patrick said. "Are you so hurt by Leo asking this Denise out that you would rather cut him out of your life? Switch tables at lunch, stop talking to him altogether."

Yvonne's horrified look answered his question. "No. Of course not."

"Then there's your answer. You can have him in your life as a friend or not at all. If this romance, this love you long for appears la—"

"There you two are."

Patrick looked up at the sound of Ewan's voice. His son and Natalie appeared at the top of the stairs.

"We've been looking everywhere for you, Vonnie," Natalie said. "What's going on?"

Yvonne sprang up from the couch, looking much happier than she had when he'd come up. He thought it looked a bit forced. Apparently, she didn't want her parents to know she was hurting. "Nothing. Pop Pop and I were just talking. I have a bunch of homework to do. Are we going home now?"

Natalie nodded and followed Yvonne down the stairs. Ewan gave him a quizzical glance, but Patrick merely smiled, feeling pleased that he'd been able to ease the young girl's mind and that she'd chosen him to confide in.

Maybe he wasn't as bad at talking to teenage girls as he feared.

Ewan shrugged when Patrick said nothing. "See you tomorrow, Pop." Then he walked downstairs, following his daughter and wife.

Patrick slipped back down on the couch, reaching for the picture frame that sat on the end table. He ran one finger over his beloved Sunday's face, speaking to her as he so often did. "Not so bad if I say so myself," he murmured.

His self-satisfaction was brief, however. Because somewhere in the back of his mind, he could hear Sunday laughing. And he wasn't sure the sound was one of congratulations. It sounded perilously close to that laugh she'd always given him when he'd been a damned fool.

Teenage girls would always defeat him.

❧   I   ☙

"Hey, hey, good lookin'. Whatcha got cookin'?" Yvonne crooned as Leo Watson walked in the back door to the kitchen in Sunday's Side, her family's restaurant.

Leo gave her a half-hearted grin as he placed a large box of produce on the counter. He handed Aunt Riley the delivery list and an invoice. "You got everything except the beans. They're slow coming in, thanks to all this damn rain."

"That's okay." Riley peered into the box. "Damn. Look at those tomatoes. Gorgeous. I have no idea what you Watson boys do to grow such beautiful tomatoes. I swear I think you've got magical powers you're hiding from the world."

Leo didn't even crack a smile. "I wish."

His subdued tone captured Yvonne's attention. Leo had been delivering produce from his family's organic farm since graduating from high school and entering the farming business full time. He and his brother, Josh, worked with their dad, who had farmed the same land with *his* father, while his mother and sister ran the farm market. Back in the days when it had been her grandmother Sunday running the restaurant, the deliveries were made by Leo's grandfather.

Leo came by twice a week with fresh vegetables, and he

typically hung out for a little while to shoot the breeze with her and Riley, or popped over to the pub to say hey to Padraig. For a few months last year, she and Leo had even taken up running together a couple mornings a week because Yvonne had wanted to lose weight, and she'd coerced him into joining her because, while he was totally fit, she'd thought it would help him manage his stress. The jogging club hadn't lasted long, both of them excellent at coming up with excuses not to run.

Yvonne had noticed he'd been a bit of a bear for the past month or two, not saying more than a few words before rushing out again. She was starting to miss him.

"What's wrong, Grumpy Gus?" she asked, pressing her shoulder into his, trying to provoke at least some sort of smile. "You doing okay?"

Leo's frown was firmly in place, as he merely nodded in response.

"You know, I was thinking," Yvonne said, starting to worry about him. Leo was always pleasant, polite, and when she managed to get him to sit still for three minutes, he was funny, great company.

Not that she'd convinced him to indulge in too many of those rare relaxing moments since they'd both left high school and started their own careers. Leo was—plain and simple—a workaholic. And while she didn't find that particularly healthy, he'd always been pretty good at juggling all the balls, so she tried to accept it as part of his nature.

"Thinking about what?" he prompted, clearly intent on heading out without even taking a minute or two to visit like he usually did.

"When was the last time you hung out at the pub with a bunch of us? I know Lochlan, Colm and Padraig would love to see you and catch up. I swear it's been at least a year since we've had the whole gang together."

"That April Fools party," Leo responded.

His answer took her aback. Had it really been that long? "Seriously? That was nearly a year and a half ago."

"I don't have a lot of free time right now, Yvonne. I was lucky I managed to make it that night."

"Make some time," she suggested. "If you don't mind me saying, you look worn out. A night with the Collins clan can cure a lot of ills. Why don't you stop by tonight after—"

"Tonight won't work."

"Why not?"

Leo sighed. "Listen, Yvonne. I need to finish up these rounds and get back to the farm. We're shorthanded and there're a bunch of crops that need to be harvested."

"You're always shorthanded," she grumbled.

"Maybe some other time, okay?"

Before she could reply or even say goodbye, Leo was already out the back door.

"Damn," Riley said, sliding next to her. "That boy is headed for a breakdown."

"He's thirty-one, Riley. Hardly a boy."

Riley shot her a look. "That's not the point. Leo looks stretched about as thin as a body can get. I'm starting to worry about him."

Yvonne nodded, turning when the timer went off to pull the large pan of shepherd's pie out of the oven. She'd been helping her aunt cook in the restaurant since middle school. She loved to cook, loved spending time here in the midst of all the delicious smells, reworking old recipes that had been passed down from Grandma Sunday to Riley, and now to her.

This restaurant was her happy place, her Mecca, her dream job. Sunday's Side was connected through a large open doorway to Pat's Pub, the business her Pop Pop had been running ever since he'd arrived in America from Ireland.

Her dad, Ewan, managed the restaurant with her aunt Keira, and Yvonne's plan for the future included cooking in the kitchen and eventually taking over the running of Sunday's Side, after

Dad and Keira retired. Her cousin, Padraig, planned to assume the helm on the pub side and was already sharing the tasks associated with running it with his father, Tris.

Yvonne had known pretty early on exactly what she wanted to do with her life, so from a career standpoint, she'd always had her shit together. It was everything else she couldn't seem to get a handle on.

"I'm worried too," Yvonne confessed. "But what can we do? You know Leo. He's a private guy and he's not the type to complain. If he doesn't want to tell me what's going on, I'm not sure how to help."

Riley shook her head. "If the mountain won't come to Muhammad, Muhammad must go to the mountain."

"Meaning?"

Riley rolled her eyes. "Seriously? I need to explain this to you? After all the years you've spent in this kitchen with me while you were growing up? Something I figure your poor mom regrets allowing."

Yvonne laughed. Her mom adored Aunt Riley, she honestly and truly did. But the women were as dissimilar as salt and sugar. Riley was loud, flamboyant, opinionated and had a tendency to pepper her sentences liberally with the "F" word. The first time Yvonne let that whopper slip, her mom had pointed at her dad and said, "I blame Riley for this."

Dad had promised to ask Riley to clean up the language around Yvonne and she could attest to her aunt's efforts to do so. Riley's cursing turning to flavorful "near misses" as she turned fuck to fudge, shit to sugar and bitch to biscuit. However, she abandoned that game when Yvonne turned fifteen because "it was too fucking exhausting." After that, she'd let the language fly, then followed every curse word with "Don't say that in front of Natalie or she'll kick my ass."

And Yvonne had managed to follow that rule...mostly. At least until after high school.

"Meaning," Riley said, shaking her head in disbelief over

having to explain herself, "you know better than to listen when people feed you a line of bullshit. Listen with your eyes, not your ears. He says he's fine, which is a bold-faced lie. You saw him. I'm pretty sure he was wearing that same shirt the last time he was here—and it hasn't been washed. The damn thing is filthy. His hair is shaggy, which is unusual for him. He's long overdue for a haircut...and a shave. He never comes in here looking all scruffy-faced like that. There are darker circles under the dark circles under his eyes, and if he's slept more than five hours a night this past week, I'll eat my bra."

"You're wearing one today?" Yvonne joked.

"Smartass," Riley said, chuckling. "That boy needs an intervention."

Yvonne considered that as Riley walked over to begin mixing the dough for the homemade bread they planned to serve with the special tonight.

Yvonne began to unpack the box of produce, putting the vegetables away as she recalled the first time she'd seen Leo look so done in.

It had been the night of graduation. Lochlan's parents had planned a blowout celebration for him and several of his closest friends, and Yvonne had been headed to her car, planning to drive to the party, when she'd noticed Leo sitting alone in the school parking lot...

YVONNE GLANCED around the quickly emptying parking lot. Most of the graduates and their families had already shared the hugs, taken the requisite seventy-two million cap and gown pictures, and headed out.

She tucked her keys back in her skirt pocket and walked over to him. "Leo?"

Though the window was rolled down, Leo didn't look up at the sound of her voice. He didn't even seem to see her approaching his truck.

She thought he looked far too depressed for someone who had just graduated from high school. If it was her who'd just busted out of this joint, she'd be dancing naked in the streets right about now. She walked right up to the driver's side window of his pickup and said his name again.

He raised his eyes, meeting hers slowly. There was utter devastation on his face.

Something that wasn't a complete surprise. He'd been subdued and...well, sad, for the past few weeks. She and Lochlan had both asked him if he was okay, had tried to cajole him out of his misery, but nothing had worked. Leo would simply tell them he was fine or offer some lame excuse for his melancholy— blaming it on nerves over graduation or stress over end-of-the-year exams.

Neither she nor her cousin truly believed his reasons, but Leo wasn't ready to tell them what was really wrong, so they'd given him space and time.

"What happened?" Yvonne asked.

He blinked a couple of times, and she wondered if he'd heard her. He was looking at her with a faraway expression.

"Leo?"

This time, her voice penetrated. He leaned back against the driver's seat, his shoulders slumped. "Oh. Hey, Yvonne."

"Everyone else is heading over to Uncle Will and Aunt Keira's house for the party. Are you coming?"

He shrugged, then shook his head. "I don't feel much like celebrating."

Yvonne hated seeing him like this, and she was tired of tiptoeing around him. Avoiding problems wasn't her style, so she crossed in front of the truck, opened the passenger door and slid in.

"Yvonne," he started, clearly intent on feeding her the same line of bullshit he had the past few weeks in an attempt to get rid of her.

"I'm not getting out of this truck until you tell me what's wrong," she insisted.

He scowled. "Nothing's wrong."

"Liar."

Leo crossed his arms, stubbornness setting in. She smirked. She could out-stubborn a mule. If he wanted to go a round or two, she was game.

She crossed her own arms, mimicking his annoyance and his posture.

When she held his gaze, he gave in a little. "I've just got some stuff on my mind. Things I need to work out on my own."

"Like what?"

"What part of *on my own* confused you?"

Yvonne narrowed her eyes. "Acting like an asshole won't budge me because I know you're not a jerk. So I'll repeat the part that clearly confused *you*. I'm not getting out of this truck until you tell me what's wrong with you."

"You'll miss the party." It was a lame last-ditch attempt. He was running out of ammo.

"I don't care. It's not like I graduated. I still have to endure another year of high school hell." She didn't really mean that. Truth was, she enjoyed most parts of high school, though she didn't think she'd like it as much next year without Leo and Lochlan there. She was going to have to find a new group to eat lunch with, and that sucked.

"Seriously, Yvonne. I made a mess of something, and I have to figure out how to fix it on my own. This isn't something you can—"

As he spoke, something in the center console caught her eye. "What's that?" she interrupted, pointing to a small ring box.

Leo quickly picked up the box and put it in his pocket. He clearly hadn't meant for her to see it. "Nothing."

"Is that an engagement ring?"

There was no way Leo would propose to Denise. For one thing, they were way too young. And for another, Yvonne had gotten the impression the couple was on the verge of breaking up. Something she and Lochlan had mused was probably what was bothering Leo.

He and Denise had dated ever since the Homecoming dance their sophomore year. They'd been called the "perfect" couple by everyone at school—except *her*, though she'd given up her crush on him at the beginning of this year when it was obvious Leo still only had eyes for Denise. Yvonne had gone out with a few guys since then and was currently dating Ricky Bernard.

"Deo"—the ridiculous couple name Lochlan had given Denise and Leo—were even crowned king and queen at this year's junior/senior prom.

"Are you insane?" Yvonne asked, when it became apparent that was indeed what was in the box. "You can't propose to Denise."

"I already did." Leo turned away from her, looking toward the school.

"What? Why would you do that? Tell her it was a mistake. You're only eighteen, Leo. What would possess you to—"

"She's pregnant."

Yvonne fell silent, her stomach clenching in panic. No wonder he'd been so quiet lately, so worried. "What are you going to do?"

"I'd planned to take responsibility for my actions. I was going to make things right."

"That's not still the plan?"

"She turned me down. Said she wouldn't marry me."

Yvonne frowned. "Why would she do that?"

"She said two wrongs don't make a right. That she wasn't going to make this whole situation worse by marrying me."

"But..." Yvonne was flabbergasted. "You two have been a couple for nearly three years. Why would she have stayed with you that long if she didn't love you?" Yvonne had never thought Denise's feelings toward Leo were as strong as his were for her, but she wouldn't tell him that. She didn't kick a dog when it was down, and this dog was *way* down.

"I have no idea. She told me she was pregnant a few weeks ago."

"You didn't use protection?"

Leo was one of the brightest boys in the school, and he didn't seem like the type who'd lose his head in the heat of the moment.

He grimaced. "Of course we did. I always wore a condom, and she was on the Pill. But she got bronchitis a month or so ago and went on antibiotics. That makes the Pill stop working, which we didn't know. And then," he looked away from her again, "the condom broke one night."

"Is she keeping the baby?"

He nodded. "Said she wanted the baby. Apparently, the only thing she doesn't want is me."

Yvonne couldn't figure out why Denise would choose to raise a baby alone, when the father obviously wanted to marry her and was in love with her. Besides, Leo was great with kids, something she'd witnessed firsthand. Her younger cousins Darcy and Oliver adored Leo. There was no way Denise couldn't believe he would be an awesome father.

"Did she break up with you?" Yvonne asked.

"Yeah."

"What are you going to do?"

Leo shifted on the seat until he was facing her. "That's what I was trying to figure out. I don't know what to do. I can't shirk my responsibility, can't walk away from her, knowing she's having my baby."

Leo was the most upright, honorable guy she'd ever met, if she didn't count the men in her family.

"Who says you have to?"

"What?" he asked.

"The baby is yours too. You have rights. You don't have to be married to her to be a father to your kid. Did you tell your folks?"

He shook his head. "Not yet. They're going to freak the fuck out."

"Yeah." Yvonne's parents would do the same if she ended up in this situation. But she also knew that they would support and help her. "You think they'll kick you out?"

"No. God no. They're not going to be happy, but they'll stand by me. Help me sort it out. I just hate disappointing them. Hate asking…"

He didn't have to finish his sentence. She knew Leo, knew how much he hated asking for help. In a school full of immature, hormone-driven teenage boys, he'd always stood out, always seemed older, always the one who had his shit together.

"They'll help you. It'll work out fine. Neither you nor Denise were planning to go away to college. So you'll work out a schedule. Raise your baby together."

Her plan didn't sound like one he cared for. "That every-other-weekend crap?" He shook his head. "That's a shitty way for a kid to grow up."

"The baby will never know anything different. What's normal for one person isn't normal for the next. As long as you both love the baby and take care of it, it'll be a lucky kid."

Leo fell silent for a long time and for once in her life, she shut up and let him deal with his thoughts. It wasn't that hard to do. She was sort of reeling herself, so she sat there, swimming around in her own head, thinking about how much his life had changed and wondering how she would handle the same circumstance.

Finally, Leo turned to her and smiled. "I'm going to be a good dad."

She grinned back. "You're going to be an *awesome* dad."

Leo looked at her—and for the first time ever, Yvonne got the sense that he really *saw* her, not as part of their group at school, but as a real person on her own. "You're a really good friend, Vonnie. Thanks."

Yvonne smiled wider, despite the tiny pang in her heart that ached at being called just a friend.

Yvonne had thought back to that afternoon countless times through the years as she'd watched Leo with his son, Vince. Aside from her own dad, Yvonne was certain there wasn't a more devoted, loving father on the planet.

"You know what?" Yvonne said. "I think you're right, Riley. I think I'm going to have to stick my nosy Collins' nose into this and stage an intervention."

Riley wiped her hands on her apron before rubbing them together with glee. There was nothing her aunt liked more than to plot a sneak attack. "Excellent. Here's what I think you should do."

❧ 2 ❧

Leo raced down the hallway of his house, cursing at the billows of black smoke filling the kitchen. "Godda—" He pulled up short when he realized his twelve-year-old son had followed him into the room.

"Is that dinner?" Vince asked.

"It *was* dinner."

Vince sighed, then sank down on a chair at the table. "Does this mean we're having pizza again?"

The fact that a twelve-year-old boy was not excited about ordering pizza proved to Leo he'd fucked up one too many mealtimes lately.

"Um," Leo said, trying to figure out what else they could order. If he had time, he'd just say screw it and take them out for dinner, but he had too many damn chores to do here, things that he'd gotten behind on.

The sound of glass breaking had him groaning, even as he hastened to the living room.

Clint was standing next to the end table, barefoot, pointing to the dog. "It wasn't me. It was Boomer. He knocked over my glass of soda."

"Why are you drinking soda? I thought your dad said no

more Coke before dinner. You won't eat your food if you fill up on pop."

Vince grumbled. "Doesn't really matter, does it? There isn't any dinner."

Leo was pretty sure he wasn't going to enjoy the teenage years with his kid. Vince was already a pretty accomplished smartass.

"I'll figure out dinner."

Clint started to move, but Leo held up his hand. "Not one step, Clint, or you'll cut your foot. Stay there while I clean up this mess."

It had obviously been a full glass of soda because the sticky liquid had managed to splash over a good third of the floor. Thank God they had hardwood or he'd be heading out tomorrow to rent a carpet cleaner. Like he had time to do that.

He returned to the kitchen to grab a dustpan and mop. As he bent over to clean up the mess, he tried to remember when he'd lost complete control of his life.

Sadly, he knew the answer to that.

Three years ago.

Everything had fallen apart three years earlier.

It had been a day just like any other day. But little did he know when he'd walked into Pat's Pub to make his delivery that he was about to have the rug pulled out from under his feet.

He'd been in the kitchen, chatting with Riley and Yvonne, when he'd gotten a phone call...

Leo glanced at the screen of his phone and frowned.

"Telemarketer?" Yvonne asked.

He shook his head as he answered. The call was from Denise's husband, Ryder Hagen, and while it wasn't completely out of the norm for Ryder to call him, it was definitely unusual.

"Hey, Leo. Sorry to bother you. Um...where are you right now?"

Ryder's tone put him on instant alert. "What happened? Is Vince okay?"

"Yeah, yeah. Vince is fine. He and Clint are both at school."

Leo blew out a long, relieved breath and fought to control his suddenly racing heart. "Oh. Good."

However, even as he said it, he knew things weren't good.

"What do you need, Ryder?"

Ryder fell silent for a moment. "Can we meet somewhere right now? To talk?"

Something was seriously wrong, something bad enough that Ryder felt the need to speak in person.

"You know where Pat's Pub is?"

"Yeah. I do."

"I'm here right now. Would you want to come here or should I—"

"I'm not far. I'll come there." Ryder hung up before Leo could ask what the hell was going on.

Ryder had been true to his word about being close. He arrived at the pub fifteen minutes later. Yvonne had been sitting with Leo at one of the booths, trying to distract him while he stressed out over what Ryder could want. The other man had married Denise two years after she'd rejected Leo's marriage proposal, and the two of them had had a son, Clint, together. He was a decent guy, and Leo figured if his son was going to spend his weekdays with a stepdad, he was glad it was Ryder.

Yvonne started to stand up when Ryder arrived.

Ryder held up his hand to stop her. "Maybe...you should..."

His words drifted away and Leo knew some serious shit had just gone down.

Ryder was his polar opposite as far as careers went. Leo was a farmer, through and through, happiest when he was outside, soaking up the sunshine and fresh air, digging in the dirt. A lot of schools came to the farm on field trips, and teaching young kids how to grow their own vegetables made him feel like he had a real purpose in life.

Ryder, on the other hand, was the stiff-collar, expensive-suit professional businessman type. He sat behind a desk all day and the only digging he did was through spreadsheets, a fate Leo considered worse than death.

But right now, there was nothing put together about the other man. His hair was standing on end as if he'd run his hands through it a million times in the last hour. He was pale, and there was a distant look in his eyes that had Leo wondering if it had been safe for him to drive here.

"I can stay if you want," Yvonne said, looking at Leo, who nodded once. He and Ryder had probably had five solo conversations in the past ten years. Most of Leo's communication about Vince was done with Denise.

The three of them sat down.

"Ryder," Leo prompted when the other man didn't speak.

"Denise is dead."

It took a full minute for those three words to sink into Leo's brain. "I don't..."

Yvonne didn't say anything, but instead reached out to take Leo's hand. He gripped it tightly in his as he tried to make the words make sense.

"She dropped the boys off at school, and then..." Ryder took a deep breath. "The police think she must not have seen the stop sign. She was sideswiped by a truck in an intersection. The truck hit the driver's side. She was..." Ryder swallowed, and Leo knew he was fighting to say the words. "She was killed instantly."

Leo wasn't sure how long the three of them sat in that booth in silence. He couldn't find the words, couldn't figure out what to say. A million emotions slammed into him from every side.

Yvonne broke the silence first. "Where are the boys, Ryder?" she asked quietly.

With each passing moment, Ryder became more of a zombie. As this new reality sank in, Leo felt a kinship with the other man, understanding that pushing their emotions down deep seemed to be a shared characteristic.

"School," Ryder said.

"Do they know yet?"

Ryder shook his head.

Yvonne glanced at the time on her phone. "School lets out in an hour. Someone needs to pick them up, right?"

Ryder nodded.

"Okay. Do you want me to help you?" Yvonne asked.

Leo was used to Yvonne's larger-than-life personality, her boisterous laughter, her anything-goes attitude. It was a trait that ran strong through her family. But right now, she sounded like their savior, the only one at the table capable of thinking beyond the next five minutes.

"Yeah. I—" Ryder ran his hand through his hair. "I don't know what to do. How am I gonna..."

"You're going to call the school and tell them I'm picking up the boys today. Vince knows me. We're buddies. He'll be okay with that, and he can reassure Clint. The two of you are going back to your house, Ryder, and you need to discuss how you want to explain this to the boys. I think you should do it together."

Leo felt the first chink in his armor. While he was sad and confused, his son would be devastated. Destroyed. He was only nine. How did Leo tell his nine-year-old son his mother was gone forever?

Ryder's son, Clint, was only seven.

They'd agreed to Yvonne's plan, and the next few hours had felt like a decade. He'd stayed with Ryder and the boys that night, Vince begging him to share his single bed. He'd held his son all night as he cried.

Leo spent the next week at Ryder's place, neither man feeling prepared to deal with Denise's funeral or their sons alone. The old saying proclaimed there was safety in numbers, but in this case, there was comfort too.

At the end of the week, he and Ryder had returned to Pat's Pub, to Yvonne, neither of them sure where to go from there.

While he and Ryder loved their sons, and were fully capable and prepared to raise them, a new concern had arisen the previous night when they'd realized the boys, who'd grown up as true brothers—closer than any two boys Leo had ever seen—tearfully asked if they were going to be split up.

"What are we going to do?" Ryder asked.

Leo shrugged. He'd spent the entire week trying to adjust his work schedule to accommodate Vince's, but there were lots of overlapping parts unaccounted for. Ryder had mentioned the same thing. Truth was, the boys' lives were going to change drastically. Leo lived in a different school district, and Ryder confessed Clint would now have to spend a great deal of time in childcare, given his long work hours.

"The answer is simple," Yvonne said, as if they were missing something entirely obvious. "Leo moves in with you and the boys."

Leo frowned and started to shake his head.

"Think about it," Yvonne continued. "Your job has you out of bed at the ass-crack of dawn every day, while Ryder works bankers' hours. I realize that means a bit of a commute for you, Leo, but it's not completely undoable. Ryder will handle the morning shift—making breakfast, packing lunches and getting the boys to school, while you're the evening shift. You can rearrange your deliveries so that you can pick up Clint and Vince from school, then you handle dinner, homework, bath and bedtime. This way, the boys get to stay together with loving parents, and Vince doesn't have to change schools. They've suffered a huge loss. I think the best thing you can do for your sons right now is keep the rest of their lives as close to normal as possible. At least for the time being anyway. Do a six-month trial run, then reevaluate."

• • •

Leo grimaced at the memory. Yvonne had thrown that "normal" word at him twice in his life, using it to describe things that were far from normal.

And yet, she'd been right.

Or at least, he'd thought so. Until Ryder got that big promotion last month at work. It required him to be out of town several days a week for training, and Leo was dying on the vine, trying to do it all until Ryder could settle into his new position. The fact the boys were out of school for summer only exasperated things. Instead of just keeping them occupied in the evening hours, he was dropping them off at day camps or putting them to work at the farm or dragging them around on his delivery runs. They were almost always with him, and each other. Which meant the noise level and ridiculous brotherly squabbles were at an all-time high.

If he had a nickel for every time one of them bitched about the other one touching him or hogging the controller or turning the channel, he'd be drinking piña coladas on his own private island by now.

He glanced around, spotting the mountain of dirty clothes that had started creeping out of the laundry room and into the hallway. There was a layer of dust on every piece of furniture in the living room, and he didn't have to see the kitchen to know that if their dinner hadn't been scorched, they would have been eating on paper plates because the rest of the dishes were in the sink.

Typically, he could handle real life shit better than this. But with Ryder gone so much and the constant distraction of the boys, and the fact he'd had to extend his own work hours because his dad had pulled a muscle in his back, he simply couldn't do it.

He stood from the floor and walked back to the kitchen, dumping the shards of glass in the trash can.

"You guys need to clean your room. The smell is getting pretty unbearable," he called from the kitchen, when he realized the two boys had started wrestling. They were giggling now, but past experience had proven that would turn to crying or true fighting before long.

"We already cleaned it," Vince called out.

Leo knew that was a lie. He'd had a hell of a time getting his son to do anything this summer. He wasn't sure if it was puberty or laziness, but he'd had enough.

"You realize I can confirm that lie in about five seconds."

Vince mumbled something incoherent, which was a good thing. Leo had a feeling if he'd heard it, he'd flip out.

He closed his eyes and groaned when there was a knock on the door. The last thing Leo needed to deal with was someone trying to sell him something. He stomped to the front door, ready to use whoever was on the other end as a whipping boy.

He was fucking done with today.

With this week.

This life.

He swung the door open—then pulled up short when he saw Yvonne standing there, smiling and holding a picnic basket in her hands.

"What's that?" he barked, feeling instantly guilty at his rudeness.

Of course, it was Yvonne, which meant she merely lifted one eyebrow, silently chastising, even as she gave him a classic smar-tass response. "You clearly never watched Yogi Bear. This is called a picnic basket," she said slowly, as if he wouldn't under-stand the words.

He narrowed his eyes. "I can see that. What are you doing here?"

Yvonne didn't bother to respond. Instead, she skirted by him into the house. She'd been here countless times in the past three years. She and her cousin Darcy were their primary babysitters whenever he and Ryder were in a pinch and needed someone to watch the boys.

"Vonnie!" Clint and Vince yelled out in unison, delighted to see her.

"Wow," Yvonne said as she looked around the place. "I'm glad I missed the tornado that tore through here. Is that smoke I smell?"

"Dad burned dinner," Vince explained.

Leo rubbed his eyes wearily...until Yvonne lifted the picnic basket.

"He did that on purpose," she lied, "because he wanted this to be a surprise."

Clint jumped up and down, skipping along behind Yvonne as she carried the picnic basket into the dining room. "What surprise?"

"Dinner. But before we can enjoy that, you boys need to help me clear off this table."

Leo had said the same thing to them at least twelve times this week—the dining room table was covered with their art supplies, Legos, and a million scraps of paper Clint insisted he needed to keep for some unfathomable reason.

Interestingly, in the face of good food, whatever significance the paper held vanished as Yvonne went to the kitchen and returned with a trash bag that Clint happily helped her fill.

Leo watched in quiet amazement as Yvonne—with the help of the boys—managed to put the dining room back to rights in less than five minutes.

Then she went one step further, opening the picnic basket, spreading a red-and-white checkered tablecloth on the table, and pulling out a meal that had Leo's mouth watering.

She'd brought fried chicken, homemade potato salad with real bacon bits in it, and a leafy salad that she'd dressed in such a way that neither boy bitched about having to eat vegetables.

The three of them attacked the food like tigers who'd just killed an antelope, while Yvonne laughed at their exuberant eating.

Throughout the meal, Yvonne asked the boys about their

summer vacation, then skillfully turned the conversation to the state of their bedroom once they were finished.

Suddenly, Vince recalled that maybe it wasn't as clean as it could be. Yvonne told them she had one last surprise in the basket, but they wouldn't get it until they'd cleaned their room.

Vince didn't look too concerned about not getting his treat, until she added, "Until it's done to *my* satisfaction. I will be checking your work."

Vince groaned. "Aw, but the room is really dirty!"

"Stop grumbling and get to it. These homemade chocolate chip cookies are going to make it worth the effort, I promise. Or skip it. That just leaves more cookies for me and your dad."

"Cookies!" Clint yelled. "I'm going right now."

Within minutes, she had the dining room table cleared again, and both boys working in their bedroom fast and furious to earn their reward.

"How did you know their room was a mess?" Leo asked.

Yvonne looked around the rest of the house and let that answer his question. The place really was a trash heap at the moment.

"So," she said, looking at Leo, "your turn." She turned away from him and headed to the kitchen, leaving him no choice but to follow.

"My turn?" he asked as he entered the room.

"The rest of this house looks like hell too. No cookies for you if you don't tackle at least some of it."

He sighed. "Shit got away from me."

She nodded, but her expression told him that response didn't get him out of the doghouse. "So why didn't you ask for help?"

The truth was, it had never occurred to him to ask her for help. He was already concerned he abused their friendship more than he should, asking her to babysit every now and again.

She studied his face. "We're friends, Leo."

"I know that."

"Friends ask for help."

Leo didn't reply. He couldn't. He wasn't made that way. He'd been raised in a family of farmers, which meant he'd lived his entire life taking care of his own. If he planted a bed of vegetables, they were his to care for, to water, to nurture, to harvest. Responsibility had been drilled into his head from the cradle.

When he'd discovered Denise was pregnant with Vince, he'd been determined to do the right thing. He'd made that beautiful baby with her, and there had never been a question that he wouldn't give their son whatever he needed to live and thrive. He and Denise had come up with a shared custody arrangement with the help of their parents, and the night Vince was born had been the happiest of his whole damn life.

From the night of graduation until Denise passed, he'd worked long hours and had even picked up some extra handyman jobs so that he could provide child support for Vince and afford to live on his own without being beholden to his parents for anything.

That's just the way he was made. Asking for help felt like the equivalent to admitting defeat.

"I didn't want to impose," he said at last.

Yvonne rolled her eyes like he was the world's biggest idiot. "Sounds like Vince isn't the only one who needs a good kick in the rear. Lucky for you, I'm here and very, very wise. I can help you."

He was actually able to grin at her joke, thanks to his now full stomach. "I'm doing just fine."

Of course those words would have held more weight if she wasn't standing in the middle of a fucking disaster zone.

"Mmmhmm," she hummed. "I can see that. Actually, you and Ryder are usually able to stay on top of stuff. I've never seen things this bad. What's been going on?" she asked as she started filling the sink with hot water and dish detergent.

"You don't have to do that," he said.

Yvonne ignored him, snapping her fingers to her thumb in classic "shut your trap" style.

He knew her well enough to know he wouldn't win this argument, so Leo picked up a dishcloth and started wiping up the counters and kitchen table. "Ryder got a promotion at work."

"Darcy told me. I think that's great. I know it's the job he's been working his ass off for."

Leo knew the same thing, which was why he felt guilty for being pissed off about being left holding the bag. "It's terrific, and he deserves it. Nobody works harder than him."

Yvonne glanced over her shoulder at him, and he could see from her expression he hadn't tempered his tone enough. "That's debatable. You probably give him a run for his money. Does this promotion mean longer hours?"

Leo nodded. "And he's had to go out of town quite a bit lately for training."

"I see."

"And my dad pulled a muscle in his back, and my brother can't do all the farm work on his own, something he's been passive aggressively letting me know for a week now. I've taken the boys out there a few hours each day, all of us pitching in when we can, but prodding the boys to work is harder than doing the damn job myself. Plus, Clint takes karate on Tuesday nights, and Vince's little league games are eating up three nights a week."

"Damn. It's critical mass here." She gave him a quick wink that told him she was teasing, but he couldn't help but hate the way he was coming across in this conversation.

"I'm not complaining," he insisted. "I'm just saying I'm busy."

"I didn't hear any complaining. Grab that towel and help me dry the dishes," she said. For the next ten minutes, she washed as he dried, and then they put everything away. And just like that, she'd somehow managed to clean his dining room *and* his kitchen.

"Things are always easier with help," she said when they were done.

"Vonnie!" Vince called from the bedroom. "We're finished. Can we have our cookies now?"

The two of them went to the boys' bedroom and Leo watched as Yvonne—true to her word—checked Vince's cleaning, helping him make his bed properly. Then showing Clint how to fold the shirts he'd merely stuffed in his dresser drawer.

The bedroom looked better than it had in years. Literally *years*. Leo was tempted to take a picture of it to text to Ryder, who wouldn't believe it. Instead, they all returned to the dining room and Yvonne pulled out a huge tub of cookies. Once again, he and the boys plowed through them, helping themselves to three giant cookies each, along with milk.

Vince wasn't the only one who was sick of pizza.

"I swear you all act like you haven't eaten in a month."

"All we ever have is pizza," Vince said, using that sullen tween tone that drove Leo crazy.

"Most boys like pizza," Yvonne mused.

Vince shrugged. "Not every night. Can you bring us dinner again tomorrow?"

"Well—" Yvonne started.

Leo stepped closer and put his hand on his son's shoulder. "No. She can't. She's already gone out of her way to feed us tonight. Come on. You two go get your showers, and then you can watch TV in your room for an hour before bed, okay? We gotta head out to the farm early tomorrow."

"Aww," Vince groaned. "We're going out there *again*? I wanted to go to the pool with my friends."

"Maybe one day next week," Leo said, trying to figure out where he'd squeeze that in.

Both boys started to head out of the room, but they stopped at the doorway, turning back to hug and thank Yvonne for the dinner and the cookies.

Leo smiled. As much as they frustrated him sometimes, there was no denying they were good boys, and he was very proud of the polite young men they were growing up to become.

"Okay. One more thing," she said, starting down the hall, clearly intent on tackling the laundry.

Leo reached for her hand, tugging her back. "I'm drawing the line there. You've already done enough, Vonnie. I can handle the rest."

"I swear you are the most thickheaded man I've ever met. Didn't we just go over this? You don't have to do everything alone."

"Seriously?" he teased. "You're calling *me* thickheaded? Let's face it. When God was handing out stubbornness, the Collins family got in line twice."

She laughed and corrected him. "Three times. But that's okay because we also tripled up on the lines where they hand out fun, humor and good looks, so it evens out in the end."

Leo rolled his eyes, perfectly accustomed to her silliness, and not completely disagreeing. He'd spent countless hours hanging out with her and her cousins in high school, and even in the years since. There was no denying they were a fun family, a direct contrast to his very quiet, very solemn one. Not that his family wasn't loving, they just didn't laugh much. Hell, they rarely talked except to discuss work.

Lochlan and Yvonne had been the first friends he'd made at school. Up until sophomore year, his mom had homeschooled him, his sister, and his brother because they'd needed help with the farm. However, when Leo—the baby of the family—hit fifteen, he'd decided he wanted to go to a real high school, and he had put his foot down. After much pleading, his parents had given in to his request.

Lochlan and Yvonne had found him wandering around the cafeteria with his lunch tray on the first day of school, regretting his insistence at attending public school when faced with finding somewhere to sit. He figured there was nothing more intimidating on the planet than a high school cafeteria full of teenagers. Fortunately for Leo, Lochlan had waved him over to their table, and Yvonne had started asking him a bunch of questions about himself. By the time lunch had ended, both Collins kids felt like old friends.

And before Leo knew it, they—and their entire family —were.

"So we're doing laundry," she said.

"You're incorrigible, Yvonne."

"What?" she asked, pretending to misunderstand him. "Adorable, you say?"

She bent over and picked up a piece of paper that had fallen from the pocket of Vince's jeans, then grinned. "Uh-oh, Dad. I'm not sure if you've had 'the talk' with Vince yet, but it appears he's caught the attention of a little girl named Delaney."

Leo took the paper from her and skimmed the love letter. "Shit. I'm not ready for this part of parenting."

"He's still young. I suspect you have a couple years before it gets really serious. Of course, once he hits high school, all bets are off."

Leo looked back down at the paper. "I don't know. Delaney has professed her undying love here. Sounds like wedding bells might be ringing in his near future."

Yvonne laughed. "I wouldn't worry too much about that. Girls fall in and out of love all the time. In fact, I was madly in love with *you* when I was a freshman."

That tidbit took him aback. "Seriously?"

She nodded earnestly.

"Why didn't you tell me?"

Yvonne rolled her eyes. "For one thing, I was fourteen, and nowhere near as confident and mature as I am these days."

Leo reached out and ruffled her hair playfully. "Not sure 'mature' is a word I'd use to describe you even now."

She knocked his hand away, feigning a scowl. "And for another reason, you only had eyes for Denise."

She was right about that. He'd been head over heels in love with Denise Flynn, his first love, his first time, his first broken heart. Sometimes he found it hard to remember the boy he'd been before her.

"You could have told me about it since then. I think it's kind of sweet."

She crinkled her nose. "It's kind of an embarrassing thing to admit no matter *how* old you are, especially since you've aged so horribly. Wrinkles, spare tire, dwindling hairline."

Leo lifted his shirt to show her his very muscular stomach. "Point to the spare tire, you wench."

She laughed and pretended to punch him. "Besides, we're really good friends, and in a lot of ways, that's better."

When he looked back, he realized she was right. She'd been there for him through literally all the good and bad times. There was no denying how much her friendship had meant to him throughout his life.

But knowing she'd had feelings for him...it suddenly opened a door he didn't even realize had been closed.

He'd always treated her like a friend because that was all she'd ever indicated *wanting* from him. He had been blinded by love for Denise during high school, which suddenly felt like a big mistake...or wasted time...or...

Damn. If he hadn't been such an idiot, he might have seen Yvonne back then as something more than just another buddy.

Yvonne leaned over again and started picking up the clothing that hadn't quite made it to the laundry room, so he reached for her arm.

"I mean it, Vonnie. You don't have to do that."

She twisted to face him, turning faster than he'd expected. Her face was angled up toward his—and suddenly they were so close, he could practically count the freckles on her nose.

Leo didn't move away, something he could see confused her... until she tilted her head curiously and moved half an inch closer. It didn't take a genius to know she was inviting him to kiss her.

Actually, she was a Collins, so that invitation felt more like a dare.

None of that was shocking. This was Yvonne after all. She was the queen of calling his bluff.

No. What *was* surprising was that he was tempted to take her up on the offer.

Seriously tempted.

And Yvonne knew it.

In fact, she confirmed it when she whispered his name, almost breathlessly, then licked her lips. "Leo."

"Yvonne," he murmured, drifting toward her slowly, until he could feel the heat from her breath on his face, could smell the chocolate from their dessert.

What would it feel like to push her against the wall roughly, grasp her wrists and pin them to it? To kiss her senseless, then strip her naked, carry her to his bedroom and tie her to his bed, where he would—

"Dad!"

❦ 3 ❦

Yvonne pulled away as Vince called out his name from his bedroom.

"Dad!" Vince yelled again. "Can Vonnie watch *SpongeBob* with us?"

She laughed lightly, pretending as if whatever had passed between them had never happened. Leo wished he could push it aside as easily, but he'd already let the fantasy play out too far in his mind, and now he was struggling to keep his thickening dick from becoming too evident.

"The boys and I sort of have a bedtime routine whenever I watch them for the night," she explained.

Leo wanted to say something to her, wanted to explain— though God only knew what he'd say.

What excuse could he offer for nearly kissing her? No—for nearly *ravishing* her? Because that was exactly what he would have done if they'd crossed that first line and kissed.

Shit. The damn woman had shown up armed with fried chicken and chocolate chip cookies, cleaned a few rooms, revealed an old secret crush, and now...all he could think with was his cock.

Obviously, he was stressed to the limit and not thinking

clearly. Or maybe it was the fact he was weary to the bone from too much work and not enough sleep. Or perhaps it had everything to do with him being fucking sick and tired of jerking himself off in the shower whenever the loneliness grew unbearable.

Then he realized he didn't want to talk to her at all. Even now, he was struggling not to draw her into his arms and give her a long, deep, open-mouthed kiss.

Hell, he was fighting like the devil not to drag her to his bedroom.

That realization washed over him like ice-cold water. This was Yvonne, not some stranger in a bar, not some woman on an online dating site.

Not that he'd hooked up with anyone in either way lately. He hadn't been with a woman in a very long time. Not since before Denise's death. Three years of celibacy.

It wasn't that he didn't want to be with a woman. It was more a combination of a lack of opportunity and the unshakable fact that he was now mother *and* father to his son. Taking a chance on dating a woman who might not love his son as much as he did had become a barrier in his mind, something he was struggling to overcome.

He wasn't sure what Yvonne saw in his face, but he'd never been particularly good at hiding anything from her.

She rose up on tiptoe and placed a soft kiss on his cheek. It took everything he had not to turn his head, changing the kiss from platonic and friendly to something full of a lot more lust. His dick twitched, and there was no way he was going to keep this erection at bay.

Until she said, "You do need my wisdom. So here's my first secret to a happy life, Leo. Don't overthink everything. Sometimes you can do something just because you want to, even if it doesn't make sense or feel practical."

Unfortunately, before he had time to let that secret sink in, she'd started down the hall toward the boys' bedroom. She turned at the doorway and gave him a sexy smile that nearly brought him to his knees. "And for future reference, I'm a hell of a kisser."

He barked out a laugh of surprise as she entered the kids' bedroom.

While she watched *SpongeBob* with the boys, he tried to distract himself from the need to drag her to his bedroom to see if she was telling the truth by tackling some of the chores. With her entertaining the kids, he didn't have to break up fights or keep Vince—who was eating them out of house and home—from hitting the kitchen for snacks he didn't need.

He'd just switched the first load of laundry to the dryer and refilled the washer when she left the boys' bedroom.

"Are they asleep?"

She shook her head. "Not quite, but I suspect it won't be long." She pointed to the laundry. "Sure you don't want help with that?"

"No. I can't ask you to do one more thing. You showed up just in the nick of time tonight. I swear I was about three minutes away from leaving all this behind, shaving my head and joining a monastery."

She laughed. "Wow. I'm not sure you could pull off bald. You have a lumpy head."

While he knew it was tempting fate to touch her again, he wrapped his arm around her neck, playfully messing up her hair. "Is that right? You really don't think too much of me, do you, Miss Collins?"

She tried to fight him off, giggling. He intended to make her work for her freedom, but her hip brushed his reemerging erection. He'd managed to will it away while he did the laundry, but it reared its head again the moment he saw her.

That was...problematic.

He released her quickly, not wanting her to see her effect on him tonight.

He'd take care of business later in the shower, and the next time he saw her, things would be back to normal, their friend-ship firmly intact, and this sudden, unfamiliar, overwhelming desire gone.

Hopefully.

"Want a glass of wine?" he asked, turning away from her to head to the kitchen.

"That would be great."

He pulled a bottle of white from the refrigerator and filled two glasses. Then the two of them walked to the living room and sat on the couch, Boomer curling up on the floor at their feet.

"Seriously, Vonnie. I can't thank you enough for dinner and helping me with the dishes and cleaning up all those rooms."

"Don't mention it," she said. "Tonight was just the beginning. I have a lot more secrets to impart."

Leo chuckled. "I don't need your secrets to being happy. I'm doing just fine."

She looked at him like he'd grown another head. "You're barely squeaking by, Watson. I'm going to teach you how to approach life like a Collins. It's a lot more fun than what you're doing now."

If she'd worded it any other way, he probably would have persisted in his argument that he was fine, but there was a lot to be said for how her family approached life. It was the first thing that had drawn him to her and Lochlan and Colm and Padraig.

For one thing, none of them seemed to know a stranger. After growing up fairly sequestered on the farm with just his parents and siblings, Leo had been starving for friends, and Yvonne and her cousins had been there, absorbing him into their circle.

When he looked back, it occurred to him some of his best times had been spent with them, either hitting the local bars or at the over-the-top theme parties they liked to throw at the Collins Dorm.

"And the first secret is don't overthink things?" he asked.

She nodded. "Let's face it, Leo. You've always tended to live in your head a little too much. Worrying about things you can't change and overanalyzing past mistakes. Sometimes it's good to be impulsive."

There were a few impulsive things he wanted to do to *her* at the moment. Of course, the fact he was thinking about them rather than acting on them sort of proved her point. He didn't have a spontaneous bone in his body.

"That could be tough for me," he admitted.

She considered that. "Yeah. I think you're going to struggle with a few of these secrets."

"Jesus. How many are there?"

"Have you met yourself? About a million! I've got a shit-ton of work to do to fix you," she teased. "The impulsiveness is actually an easy one. I think the hardest thing for you is going to be finding a way to be the truest version of yourself."

He thought about that for a minute. He'd spent a lifetime defining himself the way others saw him. A son, a boyfriend, a friend, a father, a farmer. He wasn't sure any of those descriptors defined him...not completely. Rather, they felt more like titles, roles he'd assumed for the people he cared about.

"That one might be impossible."

"Did I ever tell you about how my mom and dad got together?" she asked, her question surprising him. Yvonne wasn't the type to ever let anyone off the hook easily.

Leo shook his head. "No. I assumed they'd just met at the pub."

"Actually, my mom was a successful photographer with her own studio on the West Coast. She was doing a shoot where she followed my uncle Sky around, doing one of those behind-the-scenes biopics with a superstar, and that was how she ended up in Baltimore. Sky and Aunt Teagan were touring together by that point."

Yvonne had extremely famous relatives. Her uncle Sky was part of The Universe, a band that was often compared to The Beatles and The Rolling Stones. When Sky left the band and joined forces with Yvonne's aunt, singer/songwriter Teagan Collins, his star flew even higher.

"I swear my mom *still* can't believe I know Sky Mitchell and Teagan Collins. She shows off that autograph they signed for me to give her at Christmas all the time. The damn thing is framed and hanging in the living room."

Yvonne laughed. "They've always been Aunt Teagan and Uncle Sky to me, but I've seen the star-struck reaction everyone has whenever they see them, so I get it."

"So your mom was taking pictures of Sky," he prompted, sorry he'd interrupted her story.

Yvonne picked the tale back up. "Yep. They'd been friends for a long time, so Sky trusted her. Anyway, they were in Baltimore at the pub, and as my dad tells it, he'd had his eye on 'pretty Miss Nat' for quite a while."

"And he asked her out?"

"Sort of."

"How do you sort of ask someone out?" he asked.

"Mom was a bit prickly at the time—her words, not mine—and my dad is eight years younger than her. So she rebuffed him. Then Dad called her out for her grumpiness, and that was when she confessed she was tired of always being behind the camera, tired of being a spectator *behind* the lens while others were getting married, celebrating birthdays, anniversaries, new babies, that kind of stuff."

Leo nodded. "I get that." He'd always liked Yvonne's mother, but he'd never realized how much he had in common with the older woman. He always felt like he was just going through the motions day after day too.

"Anyway, Dad told her he'd teach her how to get a life in seven lessons."

"I'm sensing a theme here."

"You have a life," Yvonne pointed out. "Too much life. My secrets are going to help you navigate the waters and find happiness."

"Yvonne," he started. It occurred to him he'd probably made her think he was actually taking this tutoring of hers seriously, when the hard truth was, he didn't have time to play her game.

"Pop Pop has always said the fruit didn't fall far from the tree where I'm concerned. Said I may look like my mom, but I act exactly like Dad. Which means I'm persistent and hard to shake...like a bad cold."

"Sounds about right," he said wryly.

She didn't take offense. That was one of the things he liked best about her. Yvonne could dish it out, but she could take it too. She wasn't one of those overly sensitive women who was forever getting her feelings hurt. "Lucky for you, you're about to benefit from that persistence."

Leo laughed, the sound rusty to his own ears. He didn't laugh nearly enough these days. "Lucky isn't the word I'd use."

"Don't worry. Aunt Riley and I discussed all of this earlier. You're in good hands."

He groaned as Yvonne gave him a shameless wink. If Riley was involved in whatever this scheme of hers was, he was fucked. He loved her aunt Riley, but he preferred it when she turned her "attention" to other poor, unsuspecting souls.

The idea that Riley and Yvonne had plotted out a way to get him out of his funk wouldn't bode well for him. He was about to say "thanks, but no thanks" again when Yvonne stood up, crossing the room.

She pulled her phone out of her back pocket and paired it with the Bluetooth speaker on his bookshelf. She scrolled through her song list until she found what she was looking for.

He grinned when Kenny Chesney started playing. He liked country music a lot. It was one of the first things that had drawn him to Denise back in high school. In retrospect, he could see it was really one of the only things the two of them had in common.

Country music and then Vince. That was it.

"American Kids" started playing as Yvonne moved in time

with the beat. She danced back across the room toward him, her hands outstretched.

He shook his head, but she wasn't swayed.

"Dancing is a great way to get out of your head."

Leo knew for a fact that was a bold-faced lie. Dancing made him way too self-conscious.

"Leo," she persisted.

He sighed and gave in. Dancing was the least he could do, considering she was trying to help him. He held on to her hands and spun her around a few times as she giggled.

Her light brown hair flew around her freckled cheeks. He'd always thought Yvonne was pretty, in a cute-little-sister way...but he was starting to realize that kid-sister thing didn't apply anymore. Actually, it hadn't in a long time. She'd evolved from that to a close friend to...fuck, whatever this was tonight.

He'd always called her a wild spirit. She was free and happy in a way he'd never achieved.

As the music continued, he started moving his feet a bit more, laughing at her antics and the way she sang along even though it was clear she didn't know two-thirds of the words.

They must have made too much noise because both boys came sprinting down the hall, pulling up short when they saw him there—dancing. He was ready to shoo them back to their room, but he realized from the bright smiles on their faces that his stress the past few weeks had cast a pall over all of them. He wasn't the only one who needed a break.

He crooked his finger. "Don't leave me here looking like the only idiot. Start dancing."

Clint's eyes lit up, the overactive boy not needing to be convinced. He started imitating all the dance moves he'd learned from Fortnite.

Vince, however, was too much like him, more reserved, too serious. Plus, at twelve, he still wanted to act like a kid, but there was that "cool factor" to combat.

Vince's tween inclinations were no match for Yvonne,

who walked over and pulled him into their dancing circle the same way she had Leo. The two of them spun, wobbling unsteadily after they'd managed to knot themselves up. Neither of them seemed to care. They were having too much fun.

Leo started mimicking Clint's crazy moves as one song changed to another, and then another, Boomer trying to jump up on them, barking in his doggie excitement.

Nearly an hour passed and they'd all worked up one hell of a sweat. They collapsed on the couch and chairs in the living room, smiling widely.

"What a workout," Yvonne declared breathlessly.

Even Clint, who had more energy than twenty people, was sitting still, exhausted from their exertions. He yawned, and Leo realized it was way past their bedtime.

"Back to bed, fellas," he said.

He was surprised when neither of them fought him, though Vince did stop just before leaving the room to look at Yvonne. "I liked dancing with you."

Her eyes twinkled, her cheeks pink with pleasure. "Ditto, Vince. You've ruined me for all other dance partners."

He smiled and followed Clint down the hallway.

"Ruined you, huh?" Leo rose and crossed the room to her phone. He scrolled through the song titles until he found a good one.

When "Mean to Me" came on, he turned to face her, his hand outstretched.

Unlike him, she needed no convincing.

She stood up, letting him pull her into his arms as they swayed slowly to Brett Eldredge's singing.

Yvonne rested her cheek against his chest. She was half a foot shorter than him, the pixie to his giant.

Somehow it didn't feel awkward.

It felt good.

Right.

When the song ended, she stepped away. Neither of them had spoken as they danced.

"What are you thinking about?" she asked.

He looked at her for a second, trying to remember. "Nothing," he confessed. "I wasn't thinking about anything." Not the farm or his father's declining health, not the pile of laundry or Vince's bad attitude. For the past hour, he'd forgotten it all and just...danced.

"Shit," he murmured. "You're good."

She giggled with absolute delight. "Damn right, I am. The next time you're feeling super stressed out, put on Kenny Chesney and start tapping your foot a little, get out of your head and into the music, okay?"

"It's a deal."

"Well." She walked toward the front door. "I should head home. It's late."

"Thanks again, Yvonne. Text me when you get home so I know you made it safe."

He gave her a hug at the front door, resisting the temptation once again to kiss her. He worried the next time the opportunity presented itself, he wouldn't be able to hold back.

She waved, and he watched from the front porch until she got in her car and pulled away.

He returned to the living room even though there was still more laundry to be done and sat back down on the couch. As he recalled, tonight wasn't the first time he'd danced with Yvonne.

The first time they'd danced had been at Denise and Ryder's wedding reception.

Leo had wound up at the pub, pissed as fuck, after the wedding invitation had arrived in the mail. Whenever he was down in the dumps, he went to the pub. The place soothed him. Actually, it was the people *in* the place who always managed to put him back on his feet.

Yvonne, who had only been nineteen at the time, had been on her way out to meet some friends. She'd stopped when she had seen him sitting there, scowling at his diet soda, wishing he was old enough to order something stronger. He'd shown her the invitation and insisted there was no way in hell he was going to the wedding, but Yvonne had told him to RSVP that he *was* attending, then she informed him she was going to be his plus one.

He wasn't sure what sort of strange power she had over him, but he'd done as she said. Of course, he'd been no happier the night of the wedding…

LEO SAT in the corner of the hotel ballroom, watching the bride and groom slowly swaying together to their first dance. Denise had thrown the nuptials together rather quickly, the reason for this big day evident from the baby bump showing beneath her dress. She was pregnant again. Only this time, she'd said yes to the father.

Yvonne leaned closer. "Easy, Leo. You sort of look like a serial killer right now."

He didn't bother to point out he was feeling pretty murderous. She had to realize that by now.

He'd been a shitty date since picking her up, despite her attempts to keep things light and easy.

He continued to watch the newlyweds sway, his mood getting blacker by the second, until Yvonne turned her chair so she was facing him. "Look at me."

He cast her a sideways glance, then his gaze returned to the dance floor.

"No," she insisted. "Look at me. Just at *me*."

There was something in her voice that penetrated the black haze in his head. He shifted. "What?" he asked in a brusque, rude manner.

"Do you know why I told you to come to this wedding?"

He shook his head. In truth, he'd spent most of the night certain this was the dumbest fucking thing he'd ever done.

"I don't think Denise invited you to rub your nose in her happiness."

Leo didn't believe that at all.

"Leo, you want to be a part of Vince's life, right?"

He narrowed his eyes. He *was* a part of it. That chubby toddler was the best thing to ever happen to him. "Of course I do. I am."

"There are two ways to do that—one good and one horrible."

"What are you talking about?" he asked.

"You and Denise didn't work out. That's just a fact of life. Something it's taking you some time to come to grips with because of Vince. I mean, most of us break up with a boyfriend or girlfriend and it's easy to move on because we cut that person out of our lives completely. We don't see them because...why would we? Unless we're a masochist."

Leo felt the first upturn of his lips all night. Yvonne had a very logical, very funny way of explaining things sometimes. "So you're saying I'm a masochist?"

"I'm saying you don't have the option to stop seeing Denise. Every time you pick up Vince or drop him off, it's like you're pulling the scab off a wound and it starts bleeding again."

That was exactly how the past two years had felt. He didn't respond, but he nodded to let her know he was still listening.

"I think Denise hopes that by showing you it's possible to move on...maybe you'll try."

He crossed his arms, wanting to reject that idea, even though he wasn't an idiot or some heartsick fool who couldn't let go. It had become pretty clear to him in the past few months that lately it wasn't his broken heart that was causing all this resentment he felt toward Denise, it was his wounded pride. She'd said no to him and yes to Ryder. That chafed. Bad.

"Do you love Vince?"

He scowled. "You know I do."

"And you want to be a part of his life?"

"Why do you keep asking that like it's a question? I *am* a part of his life. I'm his dad. Not fucking Ryder Hagen."

"There." She put up her finger. "That right there. You can't say that."

"Why not? It's true."

Yvonne reached out and took his hand in hers. "It's not. Not really. Ryder is now Vince's stepdad. He's going to grow up with you...*and* with Ryder in his life. You say you love your son, so now you have to prove it."

Leo frowned, feeling like he'd been showing his love ever since the day his son was born. "Prove it how?"

"You have to love Vince more than you hate Denise and Ryder."

"I don't hate—" He stopped. The way he was looking at the happy couple right now, the way he'd been acting like a bear with a thorn in his paw ever since getting the wedding invitation, the cold way he'd treated Ryder every time he came along with Denise to pick up Vince, certainly gave that impression.

"You don't?" she asked.

He grimaced, and she smirked.

"You're kind of a smartass," he said, though there was no heat behind the words.

She laughed. "I'm a total smartass, and you know it."

"You're right," he said. "About all of it."

"The smartass part?"

He shook his head. "The rest."

"Sorry," she joked. "I'm not sure I heard that. I'm what? I'm *what?*"

Leo reached out and tugged her hair playfully. "You're right. Except about the hate. I don't..." He searched his feelings to be sure, but he couldn't find that emotion inside him. "I don't hate them. I'm mad and I'm hurt and...I don't hate them," he said again, the words getting easier with each repetition.

"I know that."

"So what's my next move?" he asked.

"I'm going to tell you what Pop Pop always tells me. Love is always easier than hate. If you remember that, you're golden, and it shouldn't be too hard for you because you love Vince and you want what's best for him. Kids are very perceptive. They will feel what you feel, and I can't think of anything worse than putting a child in the middle of a war and forcing them to choose sides when it comes to their own parents."

"I would never do that."

"Not consciously, but..."

But Vince would still pick up on Leo's vibes. So what was best for Vince was for Leo to put away this anger and resentment so that he could work together with Ryder and Denise to raise their son in two caring, safe, happy homes.

"Okay. I get it." It would take him a bit of time to figure out how to deal with his feelings, but he had a very good reason to try. An adorable, growing-too-fast, chubby-cheeked reason. "I'm not sure why you keep putting up with me. I haven't been all that great to hang out with the past couple of years."

"We're friends, Leo. That means we're there for each other. Period."

The first dance was over and other couples were starting to head to the dance floor.

"Come on," she said as Alabama's "Dixieland Delight" started playing. "I love this song, and I have no intention sitting at this table with your grumpy ass all night. Let's have some fun."

They were halfway to the dance floor when they encountered Ryder and Denise heading back to their place at the head table. One glance at the anxious look on Denise's face proved Leo *had* been a true asshole.

Leo stuck out his hand to Ryder. "Congratulations, man. I hope the two of you will be very happy together. It was a great wedding."

The couple looked shell-shocked for just a moment, then it was just as Yvonne had said. The whole situation that had felt unbearable a few minutes ago was suddenly easier.

Denise thanked him for coming, and the two of them chatted about how adorable the ring bearer, Vince—who was now spending the night with Leo's parents—looked in his little tux at the wedding earlier.

Yvonne congratulated and hugged Denise...

...AND EVERYTHING TURNED out exactly as Yvonne had predicted. The two of them had danced the rest of that night, laughing and acting like fools, and all the hard feelings he'd harbored toward Denise and Ryder melted away. Somehow she'd managed to take what he'd been certain was going to be the shittiest night of his life and made it fun.

She'd done the same thing tonight, swooping in to save him at a time when he'd never felt lower.

Yvonne had always been there for him, always in the background, helping him, guiding him...all in the name of friendship.

He'd spent so much of his life living on autopilot, letting circumstances and timing decide his path rather than taking hold of the wheel.

Yvonne was right. It was time he stopped overthinking things and started going after what he wanted.

And right now, what he wanted...was her.

❧   4   ❧

"Anyone up for placing a bet?" Yvonne asked as she pointed the remote at the TV, clicking through the channels until she found the baseball game. It was only her, her cousin Finn, and his best friend, Miguel, hanging out in the Collins Dorm tonight, since Colm was out on a date and Darcy was MIA.

There were four cousins currently living in the apartment where Pop Pop and Grandma Sunday had raised their seven children many, many moons ago. When Pop Pop got older and the family started to worry about a nearly eighty-year-old man living alone, Riley had added an addition onto her house and moved him in with her family. Which left the apartment above the pub empty, until the cousins began graduating from high school and college and decided to save money by rooming here together.

Aunt Riley had dubbed it the Collins Dorm, and for the past decade, most of the cousins had taken up residence there for some period of time. While Lochlan and Fiona had never lived in the dorm, Caitlyn, Ailis, Fergus, Sunnie, and Padraig had all moved out after finding love and building new homes and new lives.

As one of the older cousins, Yvonne missed the days when

there were quite a few of them coming and going in the apartment. As more and more of her cousins fell in love and moved on with their lives, she felt herself feeling a bit left behind.

Not that the apartment was quiet. That would be impossible with Finn as a roommate. The guy always had something crazy going on, and with Miguel as his constant sidekick, there was never a dull moment.

"Nope," Finn said. "None of us would bet against the O's. Besides, I've already got twenty bucks on the game with Lochlan. Asshole must have been dropped on his head as a baby. Never known a Collins to bet against the home team as much as he does."

"Gotta blame that one on Uncle Will," Yvonne said. "His misplaced devotion to Pittsburgh, just because he was born there, has really skewed Lochlan's perspective on sports."

Miguel kicked back, resting his feet on the coffee table. "I'm from New York, but you don't see me rooting for the fucking Yankees."

Finn pointed to him as if he'd made a brilliant point. "That's because you were raised right."

"Hey, where are Sunnie and Landon? I thought they were coming over to watch the game with us," Yvonne said.

"They're probably shagging," Miguel responded with an eye roll. "They're always shagging."

If anyone would know, it would be Miguel. He and Landon were partners with the Baltimore Police Department, and Yvonne got a sense that there was very little the two cops didn't talk about while on patrol.

Finn laughed. "Jealous?"

"No," Miguel said. "I mean, Sunnie is hot and all, but she's not my type."

"I meant *of* Sunnie," Finn corrected.

Miguel snorted. "Landon is straight as an arrow."

"And you're straight as a rainbow," Finn added with a good-natured laugh.

Miguel crooked a finger. "Come to the dark side, my friend. We have cake."

Miguel was bi and forever flirting with Finn, and while Finn had never dated a guy, sometimes Yvonne wondered if her cousin wasn't a little bit curious...and maybe intrigued by his friend's offer.

Not that he ever did more than brush off Miguel's flirtations as a joke.

"Nope," Finn said. "Got myself a hot date this weekend."

"You holding out on me, man? With who?" Miguel asked.

Finn shook his head. "Not telling you. Don't want to jinx it. I really like this woman. Hoping it goes well."

Miguel considered that in silence, a rarity for him, though Yvonne could tell he was dying to know who the woman was.

"By the way, where's Darcy?" Yvonne asked.

"She's babysitting," Finn replied.

"Babysitting who?" she asked.

"My rugrats," Leo responded from the top of the stairs.

Yvonne smiled when she saw him. "What are you doing here?"

"Taking you out," he replied.

Yvonne tilted her head. "Out where?"

Miguel rolled his eyes and threw his hands up. "Jesus, Vonnie. There's a good-looking guy standing at your door inviting you out. Go run a comb through that rat's nest you call hair, swipe on some mascara and get moving. If *you* don't take him up on the offer, I will. Hot country boy, sexy city cop—sounds like a match made in heaven."

She stood slowly, flipping her hair over her shoulder. "My hair is not a rat's nest. And I notice you didn't tell me I had to put my bra back on."

Leo laughed. "I'm okay with bra optional."

Yvonne twisted in surprise. "Damn, Leo. Be careful. That sounded a hell of a lot like a joke."

"Or flirting," Miguel said, grinning at Leo.

Leo's answer was succinct. "Either works."

When she still didn't move, he added, "I owe you a dinner after the other night."

"That wasn't a payback kind of thing. I like feeding you and the boys."

Yvonne didn't miss the curious way Miguel and Finn were looking at the two of them. She didn't blame them for wondering. She was in the same boat. She'd spent a fair amount of time the last few nights, tossing and turning...and failing to take her own advice to Leo. While she'd told him he didn't need to over-think wanting to kiss her, *she'd* been able to think of nothing else.

Leo didn't say anything, just crooked one impatient eyebrow at her, drawing attention to his bright blue eyes.

She'd had a serious crush on Leo her freshman year, and while that feeling had ebbed and flowed over the years as she fell in and out of love with other guys, her attraction had elevated beyond crush to outright desire after that near-miss the other night. She'd really wanted that kiss.

Miguel was right. Leo was totally hot, his looks only improving with age. He'd gotten his dark brown hair cut at some point in this past week. She loved the way he wore it short in back, but left it a little longer on top. It gave a girl something to run her fingers through.

"Give me a minute," she said, as she headed toward her bedroom. "Am I okay in these jeans?" she asked, though she knew she'd change anyway. Leo had taken some efforts with his appearance tonight. Typically, he wore faded, well-worn blue jeans and ratty T-shirts that had somehow managed to survive a thousand and three washes. Not that she expected him to wear anything different on a day-to-day basis. He was a farmer, constantly digging in the dirt. It would be silly for him to dress in anything nice, for goodness sake.

But tonight...he was almost dressed up, wearing crisp khakis and a short-sleeve navy-blue polo shirt that allowed her a peek of the ink on his upper arms.

"Jeans are fine," he said. "I thought we'd hit Mo's Seafood. You haven't eaten, have you?"

She shook her head. "Nope. We were going to order pizza later, but I'll never say no to a crab cake."

She went back to her room, quickly changing—and putting her bra back on, though she certainly didn't want to—then she freshened up her makeup and headed back to the living room, where Leo was hanging out on the couch, watching the baseball game with Finn and Miguel.

"I'm ready," she said, glad to be escaping. The Orioles were already down three runs and Finn was losing his shit, not happy about going down in a bet against Lochlan, who really did take bragging to the next level when his team won.

Leo smiled at her. "You look great."

"Thanks."

The restaurant wasn't too far from the pub and it was a lovely evening, so they decided to walk. She gave him a sideways glance when he reached for her hand.

"Hand holding?" she asked.

"You told me to not overthink it," he murmured.

She snorted. "Yeah, but I'm thinking *one* of us should give this a passing thought or two."

Leo used his grip on her hand to pull her even closer, opting instead to wrap his arm around her shoulders. "Fine. You think. I'll act."

"Dear God. That would be horrifying. How the hell would *that* work?"

Leo chuckled, then placed a quick kiss on the top of her head. "Will my very wise guru give up on me if I confess to struggling with that first secret?"

"Struggling how?"

He stopped walking, twisting her until they were facing each other. "I can't stop thinking about you. It's become a distraction."

Yvonne didn't respond one way or the other, trying to cling

to the upper hand for at least thirty more seconds before confessing she was failing in taking her own advice as well. "A distraction."

He nodded. "We're friends, Vonnie. We have been forever. I'm not sure why this is suddenly..." He sighed. "An issue."

She laughed. "So I'm a distraction *and* an issue. Take it easy with the sweet words, Leo. You're sweeping me off my feet here."

He snorted and started walking, but she noticed he didn't hesitate to put his arm around her again. She liked the way he held her close.

"Fifteen years of friendship," he murmured.

She tried not to grin at his confusion, even as her heart did flip-flops. She was distracting Leo...in a good way. "You have to remember you were in love with Denise the first four years."

"Denise and I only dated two years."

"Yes, but you didn't really let go of her until she married Ryder."

Leo nodded. "Okay. I'll concede that one. And what about the eleven years since?"

"We're going to blame that on life. I spent that year abroad, and then at least five of those years, I had a string of sort-of-serious boyfriends, and you dated that horrible Missy for the better part of a year."

Leo laughed. "Missy *was* pretty horrible."

"I choose to refer to her as your rebound. It's either that or the year you stopped using your brain and started thinking with your dick."

"Both are accurate."

"And then," she paused, always struggling to mention Denise's death. "Then Denise was killed...and ever since then, you've been busy with Vince and the farm. You've spent the last three years completely rearranging your life to see that two little boys, who've lost so much, have everything they need to be happy. So...it's just life, Leo."

Leo tucked her even closer. "You're right. In some ways, I feel like I've been absent in my own life for the past few years. Maybe even longer. I look back and can't quite figure out what I've been for thirty-one years."

"We're both guilty of working too much. But while I have plenty of time left over to go out, have fun, and do things just for me, you spend that time with Vince, like you should."

"You know, for someone who doesn't overthink things, you always seem to have the right answers."

Her eyes lit up. "Can you tell Finn and Colm that? Or maybe just write it down and sign it so I can pull it out the next time any of my cousins tell me I'm wrong about something?"

"I'm putting nothing in writing."

"Asshole," she joked. "And I'm not giving up on you just because you can't manage the first piece of advice, because..." She sighed, debating whether or not she should confess. "I might have spent a little bit of time the last few nights thinking about you too."

Leo threw a victorious fist in the air. "Yes! Caught you. So you're one of those 'do as I say, not as I do' type of people."

"Maybe I am."

They arrived at Mo's, so they curtailed the conversation until they were seated together at a table.

Once the waiter left to get their drinks, Leo picked it up again. "So why don't we put the first advice on hold for now."

"What about the second advice I gave you? How are you doing on becoming the truest version of yourself?"

He rubbed his jaw. "That one's not going to happen overnight. Although, I feel like..."

"Yeah?" she prompted when he hesitated.

"I feel like tonight might be a start."

Yvonne thought about that, then agreed. "Calling a sitter and taking a night for yourself is a *very* good beginning." She didn't add how thrilled she was that he'd chosen to spend that rare night off with her.

The waiter returned with their drinks.

"So let's move on to the next advice. Hopefully, it's an easier one. What is it?" Leo asked after they'd placed their orders.

"You need to learn how to take a chance on something even if you don't know how it's going to wind up."

Leo took a drink of beer from his pint glass. "I don't always know how things are going to end."

"Leo," Yvonne said, unable to believe he couldn't see this about himself. "You are the king of careful planning. You schedule a time to create a schedule. You have every day plotted out down to the minute. I think that's why you were losing your shit the other night. Ryder getting that promotion has jacked up your routine."

"I'm a farmer, Vonnie. We live and die by routine."

"I understand that, but sometimes it's cool to just take a risk, to throw caution to the wind."

"Is that what you did the year you were in Europe?"

She nodded. "Sort of. I mean, I had a list of the places I wanted to see, and I'd researched where the hostels were and figured out the cheapest means of transportation so I could stay longer. It was an incredible experience."

"I've always admired the way you just grab the bull by the horns. When you want something, you go for it."

Yvonne grinned. "Really? Because I don't remember any of that admiration coming my way the night of my bon voyage party. I seem to recall you telling me I was a reckless idiot."

Leo leaned back in his chair. "Well, you were that too. I was worried about you taking off on your own like that, heading to foreign countries with no more of a plan than to backpack all over creation and," he finger-quoted the rest, "eat amazing food."

Yvonne took a sip of her beer. "What can I say? I like to cook. Besides, I came back with an entire arsenal of incredible recipes and cooking techniques."

Leo's eyebrows furrowed. "I couldn't believe your parents went along with it."

"I was twenty-four years old. It wasn't like they could forbid me. Though my dad did assure me he wasn't Liam Neeson, and he did *not* have a particular set of skills if anything bad happened."

Leo laughed.

"Besides, I met up with lots of family along the way. I did Paris with Uncle Sky and Aunt Teagan for a couple weeks after they wrapped up their European tour. Stayed with distant relatives in Ireland for a while, and then Mom flew over to take that six-week cooking class in Venice with me. It was an incredible experience."

"It sounds like it."

"*You* should have come with me."

Leo closed his eyes. "You know I couldn't do that. My family needed me. Vince needed me."

"I know. I'm sorry you don't have the same freedom to roam, to explore."

"I don't want that."

Yvonne smiled. "I think maybe you do, but you'll never admit it to yourself."

"There's no point in wanting something you can't have, Vonnie."

Yvonne glanced across the table and noticed the faraway look in Leo's eyes. "Pretend."

"What?" he asked.

"Pretend you could have anything your heart desired. If you were free to go anywhere, do anything, what would you choose?"

He didn't answer, and for a moment, she thought maybe he wouldn't say. She was just about to let him off the hook when he leaned forward and rested his elbows on the table.

"I don't know what I want."

She thought perhaps he was dodging the question, but one look at his sad, bewildered face told her he was telling the truth.

Leo had never given himself the chance to dream.

Not once.

"Maybe you should think about that."

He grinned. "First you tell me not to overthink and now you're telling me I should?"

She laughed. "Let me start over. First advice is, don't overthink the *small* things. And then the next is...damn...I probably should have written all of this down."

"What?" Leo asked, feigning surprise. "You're flying by the seat of your pants here? I had no idea. Bet your dad had a list when he played this game with your mom."

She stuck her tongue out. "Advice two is find yourself. Third is take a risk. And my new advice, based on this conversation, is to dream."

He leaned back. "Dream," he repeated. "Why does it feel like your advice is getting harder, not easier? No wonder I suck at achieving a happy, carefree Collins lifestyle. Not sure how you all manage it."

She laughed. "Have you met my family? We're all insane."

Their dinner arrived, so they turned the conversation to easier things, talk of dreams and finding happiness fading away, as the comfortable, friendly camaraderie they'd shared since high school returned. He told her about Vince's laziness and his fear that puberty was setting in, and she filled him in on her cousin Fergus's new relationship with pop star Aubrey Summers.

"So now you have someone else famous in your family," he mused.

"Crazy, isn't it? We seem to be magnets for musicians." In addition to her uncle Sky and aunt Teagan, and now Aubrey, her cousin Ailis was married to and touring with Pat's Pub's former singer, Hunter Maxwell, who'd landed a huge record deal after winning the *February Stars* competition.

Once they were finished eating, Leo asked if she wanted to take the long way home and walk along the waterfront.

Yvonne was in no hurry to say good night to him, so she slipped her hand in his and they meandered along the wide sidewalks, watching the streetlights twinkle on the dark surface of the water. It was a beautiful, breezy, cool evening, a rarity for early August, which was usually humid as hell. Summer typically brought in more tourists, so the streets were a little busier than they were in the winter.

"If I remember right, you have a birthday coming up soon."

Yvonne grinned. "Yep. I'm about to be dirty thirty."

He laughed. "Not dreading it?"

She shook her head. "Nope. Age is just a number. And since I refuse to grow up, it's not going to affect my life in any way."

Leo chuckled. "Never growing up, huh? That sounds about right. Got plans to celebrate?"

She looked at him like he was nuts. "Have you ever known the Collins family to pass up an opportunity to party?"

"Good point."

"So, you wanna be my date for it?"

"Depends."

"On what?" Yvonne asked.

"On how your cousins, uncles and Dad might feel about that. I've seen their scare tactics whenever a guy comes sniffing around you Collins women. While that's entertaining to watch, I'm not sure it would be quite as funny from the hot seat."

"Are you *sniffing around?*"

Leo didn't reply, and for a second, Yvonne feared she'd misread what was happening between them. So she reached for humor, hoping to pull them out of the awkward moment.

"Well, if you're going to be a chicken shi—"

Leo grasped her upper arms, pulling her toward him in one smooth motion, and then...he kissed her.

Holy shit.

Leo could *kiss.*

Her lips softened against his, then they parted, and her tongue met his halfway. The kiss lingered, a gentle fusing of lips.

Then he pulled back to look at her.

"Okay," she said, a teasing lilt in her voice, struggling to find some way of grounding herself. "That was weird."

He shook his head. "No. That's the problem. It wasn't weird at all."

He kissed her again.

This one lasted longer and grew more heated when she placed her hands on his shoulders, her fingertips grazing the back of his neck. He lifted his hands to her hips, let his fingers slide beneath her top until he found skin. He stroked it, and she found herself wishing he would slide those hands higher, to her breasts. No, scratch that. She wanted them to travel lower, to cup her ass and pull her against him, let her rub against his cock.

Leo moved just one hand upwards, lightly pinching her nipple beneath her shirt, before he slid it back along her sides. She gasped, but he didn't offer her any reprieve. He didn't move away, didn't stop.

The sound of someone whistling nearby reminded them they were in public, and they broke away at the same time.

"You're right," she said, her voice huskier. "That wasn't weird."

It was overwhelming. Intense. Incredible.

But not a bit weird.

"I think I should get you home." He reclaimed her hand and neither of them spoke again until they were standing outside the pub, both lost in their thoughts.

Well, she would have been if her brain was functioning. Sadly, the only thing she could focus on was the way her body tingled all over.

"Want to come in?" she asked.

He shook his head. "No, I don't think I shou—"

"Leo," she interrupted his refusal, prepared to fight. His kiss had set her on fire. Going upstairs alone wasn't an option she wanted to consider. "Please. Just for a little while."

"Vonnie, if I go upstairs with you, we both know this night's not ending with a kiss, and you need time to think about what that means."

"I don't need to thi—"

He gripped her upper arms, guiding her backwards until she was pressed against the wall of the pub. She knew Leo was strong. How could he not be? The man did hard manual labor every day of his life. She wasn't sure, but she thought this move was a power play, a way for him to show her exactly *how* strong he was.

If it was meant to scare her off, he was a damn fool. She liked it.

She *really* fucking liked it.

Leo gave her a quick, rough kiss that didn't last nearly long enough, and when he pulled away, she could see he was pissed at himself for instigating it. "Dammit, Yvonne. I'm not an easy lover. If you take me to your bedroom, I'm going to pull your hair, tie you to the bed and spank your ass, then fuck you in every position I can twist you in until you've come half a dozen times and you're screaming my name. And even then, I won't stop."

Yvonne blinked several times as she let each and every one of those dirty descriptions play out in her mind. "Okay. I've thought about it. You should *definitely* come upstairs."

Leo laughed, pressing his forehead to hers. "Jesus, Vonnie. You're killing me."

"Seriously, Leo. What sane woman would refuse *any* of that?"

"Plenty of them. And...you should."

"Nope. I should not. I *definitely* should not."

"I haven't had sex since Denise died."

"Oh," she said, truly shocked. "I didn't reali— Why not?"

He gave her an exasperated look. "Because I've been busy raising a couple kids with my late ex-girlfriend's husband. Shit's been tricky."

Yvonne wasn't sure she bought that. Three years was a long time. And for the first time, she found herself questioning whether or not Leo was truly over Denise.

Leo narrowed his eyes. "It doesn't have anything to do with Denise."

"Then what?"

"Exactly what I said. I can't do a relationship. I'm committed to keeping Vince and Clint together. I can't split those boys up, and I can't see a way to add a woman to that equation. My living situation isn't exactly normal."

She rolled her eyes. "You have some serious hang-ups about what's 'normal.' Besides, you're preaching to the choir. I know all about your living situation and the boys. Hell, it was my idea for you and Ryder to raise them together."

"I made a commitment to them, and a promise to myself that I wouldn't date until they were older. The timing on this is wrong."

"Fine. It's wrong. Bad timing. Dating is totally overrated anyway. We'll just fuck, exactly the way you described."

Leo barked out a laugh and the heaviness on his face vanished for good, his smile firmly in place even as he said, "God. I need you to be serious for a second."

"That's the *last* thing you need. Your life is serious enough. So here's another secret to a happy life...laugh more."

Her quick response took him aback for a minute, but Leo wasn't the type to get knocked down. Just off-balance. "Vonnie, I shouldn't have come tonight, shouldn't have kissed you."

"Then why did you?"

"I'm...tired."

Leo didn't have it in him to lie, and she knew he'd probably never spoken truer words than those. He was further along on that second piece of advice than he realized.

But what he didn't get was there was more to it than exhaustion, and until he figured that out, he wasn't going to pursue what was happening between them.

"If you get tired again, I don't mind the kisses. They're pretty hot."

He grinned, even as he said, "I'm sorry for the mixed signals."

Yvonne knew Leo well enough to know he wasn't going to stop feeling guilty for coming over or for kissing her, because in his mind, he truly didn't see this going any further.

And though she was definitely reserving the right to try to convince him to take a chance later, she'd let him off the hook for now. She needed to gather her thoughts, figure out her next move. Aunt Riley could help her with that.

No. Actually, what she needed immediately was fifteen minutes with her vibrator. Jesus, maybe thirty. She was at critical mass on the horny scale.

Then, she'd map a course with Riley tomorrow.

Leo sighed. "I should go."

Before he could step away from her, she grasped his hand. "We're still friends, right?"

Deep creases lined his forehead as he frowned. "Of course we are. Always."

"Okay. Good. Then you're not allowed to avoid me."

One look at his face told her that while he wasn't sure where they were going from here, Leo had indeed intended to lay low for a while.

"Promise me," she pressed. "No matter what happens, the friendship remains and you don't start playing hide-and-seek. I've gotten kind of used to your grumpy ass."

"I promise. No hiding, no avoiding." He sealed that vow with a platonic kiss on the cheek that she hated. Then he turned and walked toward his car in the parking lot.

Yvonne watched as he drove away, not quite ready to go inside and deal with Finn's and Miguel's inquisition. They were no doubt both dying of curiosity about her "date" with Leo.

People came and went, waving as they entered or exited the pub, but she didn't give up her post on the wall, simply letting the world move around her.

"Yvonne?"

She spotted Kelli heading down the sidewalk toward the pub. "Hey, Kell."

Kelli was one of her closest friends, so she wasn't surprised when the other woman pulled up short and gave her a funny look. "What are you doing out here?"

Yvonne shrugged. "Just thinking. I had a date tonight."

"Oh. From the look of you, I'd say it sucked."

Yvonne laughed. "Honestly, it was an amazing date. One of my best."

Kelli digested that information, still looking confused. "My best dates usually end in the morning with me naked and wrung out after several orgasms, not with me holding up the wall of a pub looking lonely as a lost kitten, so we're going to have to beg to differ on what constitutes a 'best' date."

"I went out with Leo."

"Seriously?"

Yvonne nodded, wondering why Kelli seemed so genuinely shocked by that. "Yeah."

"Wow. Why now?"

"What?"

"The two of you have been friends forever. What changed?"

Yvonne had never told anyone except Pop Pop about her crush on Leo. And even though she'd embraced the friendship, her heart had always beat a little faster whenever he was around. She'd kept that secret buried as deeply as the feelings.

"He's going through some stuff with his family, so I took him dinner last week. He decided to repay the favor tonight, taking me out...and we kissed."

"Sounds okay so far. Which means there's more to it, because the fact remains you're standing here alone now."

"He regretted the kiss. Said he couldn't let it go any further than that because his life is a hot mess and he doesn't have time to date someone."

Kelli rolled her eyes. "Of course he does. Leo's problem is he thinks his family would fall apart without him. His parents homeschooled him, Marie and Josh so they could work the farm, and I think they still put a lot of pressure on him to keep things running smoothly. Then Denise died, and Leo gave up a lot of his independence to not only raise *his* son, but Ryder's. He's constantly sacrificing his own needs to make sure the people he loves are happy."

The reason Yvonne and Kelli were such great friends was because they were both pretty straight shooters. Hearing Kelli's perspective on Leo confirmed what Yvonne already knew. Leo wouldn't willingly date her because of his overwhelming sense of responsibility.

"So what you're saying is—" Yvonne started.

"What I'm saying is, if you want to wake up naked in that man's bed after a half-dozen orgasms—and Leo definitely strikes me as the type to rock a girl's world; it's the quiet ones who are always freaks in the bed—then you, my dear friend, have some work to do."

"Yeah, I know."

"If things work out, you wouldn't just be dating Leo. He comes as part of a set."

"Meaning?"

"Meaning, if things don't work out, if you decide to break things off, it's not just Leo's heart that could be broken. If the two of you start dating seriously, there's a little boy—actually, a couple boys—who are going to be hurt if things go south as well."

Leo had just basically said the same thing, but the way Kelli worded it really drove home his reasons for pulling back. And gave Yvonne a reason to pause, to consider. She adored those boys, loved babysitting for them. She wouldn't want to hurt them ever.

"You're right. I guess there are a lot of pretty solid reasons not to—"

"I named *one*. The boys. I'm not sure what other reasons Leo gave you. Wait—the two of you aren't playing that bullshit card about not wanting to risk the friendship, are you? I'll tell you right now, I think that's a lame excuse for not going after what you want."

Yvonne laughed. Yep. Kelli really did feel like her kindred spirit. "*That* thought never occurred to me, actually."

"Good girl."

"And you've given me plenty to think about. Thanks."

"You coming in then? I need some consoling of my own."

"What's happening?"

"School starts again in a week. I need margaritas to help me forget that fact." Kelli was an incredible kindergarten teacher who loved her students like they were her own, but like most teachers, she considered the summer months the most coveted and sacred time of the year. While Yvonne looked forward to August and her birthday, Kelli dreaded it like the plague, boycotting Target the second they put the Back to School displays out until they were replaced with the Halloween shit, which was how long it took her to get back into the swing of things.

Yvonne laughed. "Come on. Let's go order a pitcher. I'll help you drown away that pain."

Kelli walked into the pub and straight over to the bar to place their order and chat with Padraig for a few minutes as Yvonne grabbed a table and tried to sort out her thoughts.

She considered Pop Pop's advice from when she was younger. He'd said friendship and love were both important, both valuable, and she'd abided by his advice, shutting down her fourteen-year-old girl's hopes and dreams for capturing Leo's heart.

But for the first time in her life, she thought maybe Pop Pop had been wrong about something.

Friendship with Leo would never be enough.

❧ 5 ❧

Leo sat at the bar at Pat's Pub and silently chastised himself for being a fool. It had been a week since he'd taken Yvonne out to dinner. He'd seen her twice since then during his weekly deliveries, forcing himself to act natural, friendly. He had promised her after all.

Yvonne, good friend that she was, had respected his wishes and they'd returned to their normal status quo.

Just friends.

Unfortunately, none of his feelings for her these days were friendly.

Instead, they were primal, obsessive, possessive.

She'd tempted the beast from his lair and that fucker was *not* going back into hibernation.

The more she acted like "a friend," the crazier he got, and the more he wanted to drag her into the back storeroom of the pub and do dirty, dirty things to her.

Tonight, he'd hit the wall. Ryder was working late—again—so Leo and the boys had settled in, intent on watching the ball game and chilling. That had lasted about twenty minutes before Leo called Darcy and asked if she could watch the kids for a couple hours, then he'd headed here.

He wasn't sure what Yvonne had told Darcy about them, but the way his babysitter's face lit up when he told her he'd be at the pub let him know she knew enough. Darcy's last words as he'd left the house had been, "Have a good time and don't rush back. Stay all night if you need to."

Yep. Darcy definitely knew too much.

He had been equal parts relieved and frustrated when he'd arrived at the pub and realized Yvonne wasn't working tonight.

Relieved because that gave him time to have a drink at the bar and talk himself out of what he was planning to do. Without her knowing he was here.

Frustrated because if she'd been working, it would have interfered with his plans to ravish her and made it a lot easier for him to resist.

"Leo?"

Leo turned at the sound of Lochlan's voice and smiled. "Hey, man. Long time no see."

The two of them shook hands, then Leo's gaze drifted to the pretty blonde standing next to his friend. Lochlan had married his secretary, May, the two of them not only raising their newborn son but May's elementary-aged nieces as well. Leo got a kick out of seeing his "confirmed bachelor" buddy knee-deep in the family scene.

"Hi, Leo," May said. "It's nice to see you again."

"You too." Leo took a peek at the baby in her arms and smiled, trying to remember when his grumpy tween, Vince, was that tiny.

May excused herself to chase down her nieces, who'd headed straight for the kitchen to see Riley upon arrival. "I better go grab the girls before Riley stuffs them with bread and cookies, or they won't eat their dinner."

"We were just about to head over to Sunday's Side. Meeting up with Pop Pop for dinner. Want to join us?" Lochlan asked. "The more, the merrier."

Leo shook his head. "No thanks. Ate with the boys before

heading over here for a quick drink. I can't hang out too long. Ryder's working tonight, so Darcy's watching the kids."

"I'm glad to see you taking some time for yourself. You don't do that enough."

Leo wondered how Lochlan would feel if he found out he wasn't here for a break, but for Yvonne.

Actually, he was certain Lochlan wouldn't mind Leo asking Yvonne out at all. At least not until he recalled Leo's penchant for bondage, something they'd discussed one night after a few too many bourbons at a friend's bachelor party.

Then his friend might have a few words to say.

"Yvonne has been telling me the same thing, so tonight I thought I'd give it a try, see if this relaxation thing everyone raves about is all it's cracked up to be."

Lochlan slapped him on the back. "It really is good to see you. I'm sorry we haven't had a chance to go to a game together or meet for a beer."

Leo smiled. "We're *both* old family guys now. But I wouldn't mind catching a Ravens game with you when the season starts back up, if you think you can get away one Sunday afternoon. Ryder can get us pretty good seats."

"It's a plan."

He and Lochlan said their goodbyes, then Leo resumed his seat and picked up his beer. He glanced toward the closed door that led to the Collins Dorm. He'd seen Yvonne's car in the parking lot, so she was clearly upstairs.

"You waiting for someone to come down?" Padraig asked, leaning on the counter in front of him.

Leo shook his head. "No. Just me tonight." He glanced toward the door again.

"Yvonne is the only one home, if you were wondering," Padraig said, clearly noticing where Leo's attention was focused.

He nodded, distracted by that information. She was upstairs and she was alone.

Which meant he was fucked.

Meanwhile, Padraig looked in the opposite direction, to where a woman was tapping away fast and furious on her laptop.

"Who's that?" Leo asked, curious about the pretty woman. She'd been sitting there since he'd arrived, and from the open notebook beside the half-empty plate next to her, it was apparent she'd been there awhile.

"Emmy. She's a writer. Been coming in here the last few weeks to work on her book. Not sure what it's about. She won't say," Padraig replied, raising his voice so she could hear him.

"Don't want you stealing my plot," Emmy said, grinning widely without looking up. Her fingers continued to fly across the keyboard.

Her secrecy had obviously sparked Padraig's curiosity. Leo got a sense the two of them had had this conversation before.

Padraig turned his attention back to him. "Since Emmy won't divulge *her* secrets, I'll ask you, Leo. What are you doing here?"

"Can't a guy just hang out and have a beer, chat with an old friend while he's tending bar? I thought you might like the company."

Padraig rolled his eyes. "I do like the company, and of course a guy can do that. But you're not that guy, and that's not why you're here."

Leo started to glance toward the door to Yvonne's apartment, but he winced and stopped himself. It didn't matter. It was too late.

Padraig snorted as if to say "I told you so."

"I've spent the last week trying to stay away from here. From *her*." Leo didn't say Yvonne's name. It wasn't necessary. Padraig was pretty damn astute, plus, unlike Emmy, the Collins family was shit at secrets. What one knew, they all knew.

"Staying away, huh? How's that going for you?" Padraig asked with a grin. Padraig's perceptiveness was what made him such a great bartender. He had an innate ability to really listen as his patrons talked, but more than that, he could see the things they didn't say. It was one of the main reasons Leo had detoured here before heading upstairs.

"I'm sitting right outside her door, so I'll let you figure that out."

"So go upstairs."

"I'm not sure it's that simple."

Padraig tossed a towel over his shoulder. "Everything is that simple, bro."

"Dammit, man. I just got my life somewhat settled."

Padraig grinned. "That's always the time when life throws you a curveball. Wouldn't want you to get too comfortable."

"Yeah. Well, I've got a lot more to think about than just getting laid."

Padraig narrowed his eyes and seemed to grow six inches taller. "Are you going up there for a booty call?"

Leo raised his hands in surrender. "Come on, man. You know me better than that. I would never use Yvonne for sex. It's just... when Ryder and I decided to do the roommate thing, to raise the kids together, we knew what that entailed."

"What it entailed?" Padraig asked, confused. Then, under-standing dawned. "Are you saying you both swore off women forever?"

Leo shook his head. "Not forever. Well, maybe Ryder did. He'd just lost his wife, and I doubt he thought he would ever find—"

He stopped mid-sentence. Padraig's beloved wife, Mia, had passed away two years earlier of a brain tumor.

"Sorry," he murmured.

Padraig nodded, acknowledging Leo's apology. "I get what you're saying, and you're right. I'm sure when you two set up house together, Ryder did so thinking that was good enough for him. He probably couldn't see himself falling in love again."

Leo had lived with Ryder for three years, and during that time, they'd become pretty good friends. Despite that, Leo got a sense that Padraig understood the other man even better. "He hasn't changed his mind on that."

Padraig considered that information. "He hasn't changed his mind *yet*. That doesn't mean he won't meet someone who makes him consider giving love another try."

There was something about the way Padraig said it that made Leo think perhaps the bartender was talking about himself. Leo sincerely hoped so. His friend had been lonely since losing Mia. Padraig wasn't meant to live life alone. The guy had a heart as big as New York, and if anyone was cut out to be a dad, it was Padraig.

"The first year was rough on all of us—on Ryder and the boys. Your aunt Lauren was great with Clint and Vince. She really helped them come to grips with losing their mom."

Padraig's aunt was a psychologist and amazing with kids. Leo was fairly certain that without her doing counseling sessions with the boys, they would have been completely screwed up. Ryder had been dealing with his grief on his own, and he'd gone very, very quiet, working long hours before coming home, only to vanish into his bedroom. Those first months after Denise had passed reminded Leo a lot of the past few weeks, with Leo doing the lion's share of the work while Ryder was...absent.

"You always sell yourself short, Leo. You've been the glue holding your unusual family together since Denise's death. Taking care of everyone, making sure their lives could continue as normal as possible. You took a lot on your shoulders."

Leo shrugged, uncomfortable with Padraig's praise. He did what needed to be done. No more, no less.

"What you *didn't* do was swear off relationships. I get that you take your responsibilities seriously, but, man...that load seems to be getting pretty heavy. You keep going the way you have been, and it's going to crush you."

Leo realized his friend was right. He did feel weighed down. "That feeling goes away when I'm with Yvonne."

Padraig grinned. "Then why are you sitting down here with me?"

A soft chuckle drew Leo and Padraig's attention toward the end of the bar, where Emmy was still sitting. She averted her eyes as soon as they looked in her direction. She'd clearly been listening.

"You agree with that advice, Em?" Padraig asked.

She never looked up as she started typing. "I do."

Padraig focused on him again. "You should never throw away a chance at finding love, Leo. It's sort of like spitting right in Karma's face."

It occurred to him that Padraig had just given him one of Yvonne's secrets to happiness. "Well," Leo said, standing up slowly. "I wouldn't want to piss off Karma."

Padraig waved him off when he tried to pay for the beer. "Stop stalling. Get up there."

Leo walked upstairs. Yvonne wasn't in the living room, and it occurred to him as he stood at the top of the stairs, this was probably the quietest he'd ever heard the apartment. Typically, the place was full of Collinses, with the TV on or music playing.

"Yvonne?" he called out.

"Bedroom," she yelled back.

Shit.

He waited for a second, hoping perhaps she'd come out. Keeping his hands off her was going to be hard enough without having a bed just a few feet away. He was only human after all.

When she didn't emerge, he headed down the hallway. She and Darcy each had their own rooms on this floor, while Finn and Colm had bedrooms one more floor up.

Her door was open, and she was lying on her back on her bed, reading a book. He knocked on the door, leaning against the frame.

Her eyes widened and she sat up. "Oh! Leo. I'm sorry. You sounded just like Colm. What are you doing here?"

"I wanted to see you."

"Is that so?" She was obviously delighted that he'd caved.

"I *needed* to see you."

She tilted her head playfully and held her hands up. "Well, here I am, friend."

And just like that, she'd thrown down the gauntlet.

Leo shut the door and walked to her bed, pressing her to her back and following her down, caging her beneath him.

"I need you," he whispered before lowering his head to kiss her.

Yvonne offered no resistance as he claimed her lips and her mouth, deeply, thoroughly. It had been too long since he'd kissed a woman, and try as he may, he couldn't recall ever getting so turned on by the mere touching of lips.

He forced himself to break away, just for a moment. He hadn't intended to come in here and jump on her like a thief in a dark alley.

"Yvonne—" he started.

"No," she interjected. "We don't have to talk about this. I know what you want, and you know what I want. It's the same damn thing."

Leo didn't bother to correct her because she wasn't wrong. Instead, he kissed her again.

Yvonne's hands ran along his chest, then she reached beneath his T-shirt, her fingers gliding over his bare skin.

He wanted to draw this out, make it last, but he'd never succeed. It had been too long and she tasted too sweet. He reached back and grasped his T-shirt, tugging it over his head with one quick pull.

Yvonne wasted no time exploring his newly exposed parts, lifting her head to run her tongue over his nipples, her hands gripping his upper arms. She was as hungry as he was, neither of them managing to show any restraint.

He pulled away, kneeling next to her. "Sit up, Vonnie."

She did so, and he pulled her T-shirt off as well, grinning when he saw she wasn't wearing a bra.

Yvonne rolled her eyes at his delight. "It's the first thing that goes as soon as I get home."

"Not going to hear any complaints from me." Leo ran his fingers through the valley between her breasts, then cupped one. Her nipples were tight and hard and begging for his mouth.

He bent his head, sucking one in for just a second before his phone pinged.

"Shit." He reached into his back jeans pocket, intent on turning the thing off and setting it on her nightstand.

One glance at the screen showed a text from Vince—Leo was still kicking his own ass for giving in to the boy's request for a cell phone. He would have ignored the text, but the message was brief. And alarming.

I'm bleeding.

Leo twisted to sit on the edge of the bed. "I'm sorry, Yvonne. I have to…"

She sat up and read the screen over his shoulder. "You better call him."

Leo dialed his son's number. "Vince? What's happening? What do you mean, you're bleeding?"

"Promise you won't yell."

Leo hated sentences that started that way because he always wanted to yell. "Vince," he said, infusing as much warning into his tone as possible. "What did you do?"

"I was playing with your pocket knife."

"Why?"

"We read *The Outsiders* in school, and I was showing Clint—"

"Forget the why. We'll talk about that when I get home. Where's Darcy?"

"She's in the kitchen making us popcorn. We're gonna watch a movie."

Leo rubbed his eyes. "Do you need stitches?"

"No."

"Is it still bleeding?"

"No. It stopped now."

Leo counted to five in his head. "Show it to Darcy and get a Band-Aid if you need one."

"Okay."

"And, Vince...don't text again unless you cut off a finger."

"How can I text without a finger?" Vince replied. His kid had inherited his same smart-ass dry wit.

Yvonne laughed even as she chastised him. "Leo."

"Go watch the movie and don't do anything else stupid. We'll talk about the knife when I get home."

"Yes, sir," Vince said. "Bye, Dad."

Leo hung up and silenced his phone, placing it on Yvonne's nightstand.

"Sorry about th—"

Before he could finish his apology, Yvonne shifted, straddling his lap to kiss him. He lifted his hands to her breasts and pinched her nipples, loving her soft gasp that morphed to a groan when he did it again.

"Harder," she urged.

"Vonnie, baby..."

Yvonne's hands were on his shoulders and she was rubbing against him, the sexiest dry hump in history.

Leo needed to slow things down or this interlude was going to be over before it even started.

He gripped her hips, holding her tightly to stop her motion. Yvonne didn't seem to notice. She pressed her lips against his neck, her tongue roaming along his skin as her hands drifted lower, reaching for the button on his jeans.

He chuckled as he tugged her hands away. Yvonne wasn't deterred, reaching for him the second he let go.

He grasped her wrists again, only this time he held on. "Slow down."

She shook her head. "No."

"Baby, you gotta slow down."

"Not this time. *Please.*"

Leo had a list as long as his leg of things he wanted to do to her, but right now, nothing sounded more perfect than a fast and furious fuck.

He needed her too fucking bad.

He lifted her from his lap, then stood up. With her hands free again, Yvonne reached for his jeans a third time.

He stepped away. "Take off your pants, Vonnie."

She paused for a moment, but Leo's patience was gone. If she wanted a quickie, then by God, that was what she was getting.

He untied the drawstring on her lounge pants and pushed them down. Apparently, her panties had been shed with the bra. Two pieces of clothing and she was completely naked.

He'd never seen anything more beautiful in his life. Yvonne had a tiny waist that was accentuated by her full round ass and D-cup breasts. A shapely hourglass.

He'd always tried to be a gentleman and not let his eyes linger whenever their group of friends went to the pool in the summer —out of respect for her, and because her male cousins would have given him shit for it. But of course he'd noticed her in her bikini, always found her extremely attractive.

Right now, she took his breath away.

Yvonne usually straightened her hair, but she'd clearly showered before he arrived and had let it dry natural, so her long light brown tresses curled around her face and over her shoulders.

"You should always wear your hair like this," he murmured, wrapping several strands around his finger. "I like the curls."

"It would definitely be easier to do this way. My mom says I spend too much time in front of the mirror."

"You're gorgeous, Vonnie."

She smiled, her freckled cheeks flushing slightly.

Leo guided her back to the bed. "Lay down and open those pretty legs of yours."

"Oh," she breathed. "God. Yes!"

He unbuttoned his jeans, but stopped there when Yvonne assumed the position he'd requested and did his command one better by cupping her own breasts, holding them up.

She was a goddamn sex kitten.

He placed one knee on the bed next to her, intent on giving her a much more intimate kiss—

When his phone buzzed again, a call coming in. He'd turned off the sound, but hadn't silenced it completely.

He didn't look at the screen this time. Instead, he just pressed the button on the side to send the call to voicemail.

Then he turned back to her.

"Your jeans," she said.

He shook his head. "Not yet." He knew himself well enough to know nothing would stop him from sliding into her once he was naked. And while a quickie was still tempting, now that she was lying there, looking up at him with those bedroom eyes, he'd managed to get a grip. It was a tenuous one, but a grip just the same.

Leo shifted lower on the bed and ran his fingers along her slit. Yvonne's legs parted farther for him and he took advantage, rubbing her clit with his thumb. She was still holding her breasts.

"Pinch your nipples for me, Vonnie. Get them good and hard because I'm going to suck on them all night."

She did as he asked, but it was a half-hearted attempt, as she was too focused on what he was doing.

He knew how to help her remember.

Her hands stilled when he stopped stroking her clit and her closed eyes opened, lifting to his.

"I *said* pinch them."

He'd warned her he wasn't an easy lover, but the commanding tone of his voice didn't seem to alarm her. Especially when she gave him a sultry smile and pinched hard enough to provoke her own breathy groan.

It appeared he'd met his match in the bedroom. Thank God.

Leo leaned down and ran his tongue along her slit.

Her back arched, so he gripped her thighs, holding them

against the mattress. "One night, I'm going to tie you down, spread-eagle, and play with you for hours."

He ignored the sarcastic voice in the back of his head that asked, *Yeah right, when will you ever have hours?*

"I have scarves over there," she said, jerking her head toward her dresser. "And a bit of time to kill right now."

Leo actually considered it for a second, but resisted. While he'd regained some control, he'd never have the patience for that type of play tonight.

He licked her again, then pushed two fingers inside her.

"God!" she cried out. "Leo."

He pressed in and out, about to add another finger, when his phone started buzzing again.

He ignored it completely. A bomb could explode outside and he still wouldn't stop. Nothing on the planet mattered right now except fucking her until they were both lost to oblivion forever.

Then he'd do it all again.

He added a third finger, curving it and finding her G-spot.

She jerked roughly, and he knew she was close. So close.

Ordinarily, he liked to make sure his lovers came a couple times before he slid in, but he wanted the two of them to come together their first time. He didn't consider the reason for that too closely at the moment.

He withdrew his fingers, prompting her to curse.

"Goddammit, Leo!"

He chuckled as he rose from the bed and started unzipping his jeans.

"Are you fucking kidding me?" Yvonne did not like having to wait for her treat.

Leo stopped mid-zip and put his hands on his hips. "Keep it up, Vonnie, and I'll leave you hanging on the edge of an orgasm all night."

She didn't relent. "I was right there. One more little stroke and—"

"You'll come when I tell you to, and not a second before."

Her narrowed eyes told him right then and there, he and Yvonne were going to set the bedroom on fire. Her spunky challenges spoke right to the heart of his caveman-like alpha, something that would have been problematic if he wasn't completely sure she loved his demands and would enjoy his "punishments" just as much.

"Here's another piece of advice for you," she said. "Women can come more than once, so you should let them. Oh," she continued smugly, "and it's not necessary to have a man around to do it for them."

She only managed to push one of her own fingers inside before he had both her wrists in his hands and pinned to the pillow by her head.

"That's *my* pussy now, and I say you aren't coming without me. We can do this the easy way or the hard way, Vonnie. The easy way is, you do what I say without question."

"And the hard way?"

"I toss you facedown over my lap and spank that cute little ass of yours until you can't sit down tomorrow.'"

"I'm sorry, but I still haven't heard the hard way yet."

He laughed. Loudly.

Goddammit.

He took sex very seriously, and humor had never entered the equation. It was always intense. Powerful. Passionate.

But never...*fun*.

Leave it to Yvonne to knock him off-balance in the bedroom and introduce him to something he didn't even know he'd been missing out on.

Of course, he shouldn't be surprised. Heaven knew she'd been throwing him for a loop the past couple of weeks.

"You're asking for it, baby," he said, trying—and failing—to evoke a warning with his words.

"You're right. I am," she said with a saucy wink. "Hurry up."

He tugged on her wrists, intent on giving her exactly what she wanted, his fingers itching to spank her, but before he managed to do more than pull her to a sitting position, there was a knock on her bedroom door.

Leo had closed the door, but he hadn't locked it.

Yvonne quickly pulled her T-shirt back on as she called out, "Who is it?"

"It's Padraig. Listen, I'm really sorry to interrupt you, but... Leo, are you in there?"

Padraig knew he was.

"Yeah," Leo called out. "Give us a second."

Yvonne pulled her lounge pants back on as Leo walked to the door and opened it. Padraig stood in the hallway. When he saw Leo was shirtless, he grimaced. "Your brother's been trying to reach you. When he couldn't get you, he contacted Ryder, who told him you were here, so he called the pub. Leo...your dad has had a heart attack. He's at Hopkins right now. Josh thinks you should get over there as quick as you can."

It took a second for Padraig's words to sink in, but once they did, Leo flew into motion. Yvonne had already retrieved his shirt from the floor, handing it to him.

Padraig rubbed his hands on his jeans, then said, "I need to get back down to the bar. I left Emmy keeping an eye on things."

Leo nodded, silently acknowledging Padraig's "I'm sorry, man. Hope everything is okay," as he left Yvonne's room and went back downstairs.

"Leo," Yvonne said when he dug his truck keys out of his pocket, terrified that he wouldn't make it to the hospital, that he might not have a chance to say goodbye to his dad.

Fuck Karma.

He was the one who'd just gotten spit at.

"Do you want me to—" she started.

"No," he stopped her. He knew she was going to offer to come with him. He didn't want her there, didn't want her to see him fall apart.

He was barely holding it together, and the sound of her voice pierced something inside him, shattering it, the shards cutting him deep.

She made him feel too much.

Fuck it.

It was *all* too much. All of it.

"I should never have started this, Yvonne." He forced himself to look into her pretty eyes. "This is what I was trying to tell you. My life is constant chaos."

"I don't care about th—"

"I care. I have too many responsibilities, too many people relying on me. I'm already pulled in too many directions. I can't add anything else to the mix right now. It wouldn't be fair to you."

"Leo. Wait—" she started again.

"I have to go. I'm sorry, Yvonne, but I think it's better for both of us if we just stay friends. It's all I have to offer you. All I'll *ever* be able to offer."

Then, he took the coward's way out, leaving before she could respond.

$\maltese$ 6 $\maltese$

Yvonne listened as Leo's footsteps pounded down the stairs. She stood in the middle of her bedroom, staring at the rumpled comforter on her bed.

He'd come to her. On his own.

After their date last week, she'd discussed her next move with Aunt Riley, who said nothing drove a man crazier than getting what he asked for.

Yvonne had agreed to give her aunt's advice a try, returning to the *just friends* status Leo had claimed to want.

She'd almost caved tonight, tempted to grab her car keys, drive to his place, and seduce the hell out of him. Then Leo had called Darcy.

Darcy had been certain that meant Yvonne's plan had worked, that Leo was going to her. Darcy had even texted to say he was coming to the pub. But then, too much time passed and Yvonne began to question whether or not he'd ever cave. In a fit of annoyance, she'd picked up a dirty book, casting herself and Leo in the roles of the main couple, figuring that was the only way she was getting laid tonight.

Then...he'd shown up, stripped her naked, pushed her to the verge of an orgasm.

And now...

Yvonne blinked quickly, trying to combat the tears threatening to fall. She wasn't going to cry.

No crying, she repeated to herself.

She caught sight of the messy bed again.

"Fuck it," she said. "I gotta get out of here."

She pulled off her T-shirt and lounge pants, and put on a bra, panties, jeans and a clean T-shirt, grabbed her car keys, then headed downstairs.

Riley and Pop Pop were sitting at the bar with Padraig, who had clearly filled them in on Leo's hasty departure.

"Good for you," Riley said when she saw her with keys in hand.

"What?" Yvonne asked, confused.

"You're going after him, right?" Riley asked.

Yvonne shook her head. "I don't think I should. He's with his family now. That's not really my place."

"What's with the keys then?"

"I was just going to take a drive. Try to clear my head."

Riley rolled her eyes. "I don't know who's stupider about all this—you or Leo."

Padraig chuckled. "Always there with the stellar pep talk, Aunt Riley."

Yvonne glanced at Pop Pop. "I thought you were having dinner with Lochlan."

"Came over to check the score on the game." Pop Pop reached out to touch her cheek consolingly when Yvonne climbed onto the barstool next to him. "All these years. It's still him, isn't it? It's *always* been him."

"Always?" Padraig asked.

Yvonne nodded. "Yeah. I've had feelings for Leo for a long time."

"I didn't know that."

If Yvonne wasn't feeling so crappy, she might have laughed at Padraig's tone. It was very rare that anyone ever pulled the wool over his eyes.

She shrugged. "I kept it a secret for the most part. Riley's right. I'm not getting any smarter when it comes to Leo. He said all he has to offer me is friendship. And I know I should be okay with that, Pop Pop...that it should be enough for me, but—"

"Enough for you?" Riley interjected. "What the hell are you talking about?"

"Friendship is just as important as love. They're both gifts, both things to be treasured. It's better to have Leo as a friend than not at all."

"What kind of bullshit is that?" Riley asked.

"Language," Pop Pop murmured.

Riley ignored her father. "You're being a coward, Vonnie."

Yvonne looked at Pop Pop, who shifted uncomfortably on his stool, clearing his throat but not speaking.

"Wait," Riley said. "Did *you* say all that stuff to her, Pop? I've *never* heard you tell someone not to take a chance when it comes to love."

"In my defense," Pop Pop said, "Yvonne was fourteen when I offered that advice, and Leo had just asked someone else to the homecoming dance."

Riley rolled her eyes and scoffed when Padraig laughed. He turned briefly and glanced down the bar. Yvonne followed his gaze to a pretty brunette sitting at the end, who was typing fast and furious on her laptop. Then the other woman looked up as if feeling Padraig's gaze and gave him an amused grin, letting Yvonne know they had an eavesdropper.

Great.

"Well, you made this mess, Pop, so fix it. Give her the *good* advice this time. I gotta finish up a couple things in the kitchen. We'll leave for home once you've fixed your mistake. The poor girl has wasted years on this crush." And with that, Riley rose and returned to the kitchen.

Padraig gave her a quick wink, then meandered down the bar toward the woman with the laptop.

Pop Pop grimaced. "I *am* sorry, lass, for guiding you wrong."

Yvonne shook her head. "You weren't wrong. It's the timing on me and Leo that's always been wrong. Still is, apparently."

"Is that what your young man thinks?"

She nodded. "He said his life is constant chaos, and he's trying to spare me from having to deal with all that."

Pop Pop gave her an astonished look. "That's the craziest thing I've ever heard. Why, Sunday and I raised seven kids in an apartment above a pub. If that's not chaos, I don't know what is. What's more, I wouldn't trade a single one of those insane lost-homework, boys-fighting, broken-lamp days for the quietest, most relaxing, sleepy-eyed day on a fishing boat. Chaos is what makes life worth living."

"I've tried to tell him that, but he's one of those chivalrous types, trying to save me from what he considers his own disasters."

"Sounds like he needs you."

Yvonne closed her eyes against the tears forming again. She wished he *did* need her. The problem was...Leo had been making it pretty much on his own since the beginning.

"And you need him."

"I want him," Yvonne clarified.

"No, from the look on your face, I'd say you need him as much as he needs you. You're lonely, aren't you, my graceful girl?"

Yvonne started to shake her head. It was impossible to live in the Collins Dorm, to work in the pub, and still be lonely. Then she realized he was right. "I look at Leo and see a future that..." She stopped, uncertain how to explain.

She should have known Pop Pop would get it without the words. "I know the last few years have been hard on you, even if you haven't thought so. Watching Caitlyn, Lochlan and Sunnie find their paths, their loves. Your future isn't settled, though I think you'd desperately like for it to be. This young man, he's the one who's won your heart?"

"He's so honest and trustworthy and kind. Leo is a good man, who puts his family and friends first. And he's the most incredible father. You should see him with Vince, Pop Pop. The way he's raised his son is just...I think he's probably a lot like you were with your sons when they were younger."

Pop Pop smiled, and she got a sense he was recalling those years. "There is no greater thing on Earth than being a father... unless it's being a grandfather."

Yvonne smiled and placed her hand on top of his wrinkly one, trying to ignore the fact that he seemed to shrink a little bit more with each passing year. When she was a child, her Pop Pop reminded her of a giant, a larger-than-life man, stronger than a bear.

She pushed aside thoughts of him aging.

"I was there, you know," she said. "The night Vince was born. Leo called and asked if Lochlan and I would come sit with him. Denise hadn't been comfortable having him in the delivery room, so her parents were with her instead. I think it hurt him, knowing that his son was being born, and he couldn't be there to see it."

"I didn't realize you and Lochlan had been there for him. That was very kind of you."

"It was a pretty long labor, close to fourteen hours. Lochlan and I kept taking turns, running out for food and stuff. Leo wouldn't leave the waiting room. I swear he must have walked a thousand miles around that tiny room. And then, just like that, the baby was there. A nurse called us into a different room, and she put Vince in his arms. I've never seen a look like that. It was the most powerful love I've ever witnessed. I want that for my own children, want *him* raising them with me, loving them."

"And," Pop Pop prodded.

"And...me."

"I was wondering if you were going to get to that part. Loving a man because he's a good father is a wonderful thing, but it's not the only thing."

"No. It's not. And I hope you don't think I've been pining for him for years on end. I haven't. We've both lived very full, very busy lives. And the timing has always been just a little off. Until last week."

"Last week?"

"He kissed me. And..." Yvonne flushed, slightly embarrassed by her admission.

"I've done a fair bit of kissing in my life, lass. Can I assume you liked kissing him?"

"I've been falling in love with Leo in bits and pieces ever since I was fourteen. But when he kissed me...that was it for me. Hook, line and sinker." Her Pop Pop loved fishing, so she knew he'd appreciate the metaphor.

"Well, then, I think the answer is obvious."

Yvonne sat there for a moment, trying to recall the question. "It is?"

Pop Pop nodded. "Go to the hospital. Your place is there. With your man."

"My man?" she asked, teasing. "Not my friend?"

"My dear girl, if you have an ounce of compassion, you will forget that terrible advice, and perhaps do an old man a favor and not tell anyone about my brief lapse in judgment. I do have a reputation to uphold in the family."

Yvonne laughed, leaning forward to kiss her grandfather on the cheek. "I won't say a word. I won't have to. Twenty bucks says Riley didn't have a damn thing to do in the kitchen. I suspect she's already managed to call at least three of her six siblings to tell them the story."

Pop Pop grimaced. "I never take a bet I won't win. I suspect you're right. So you go to Leo and show him that a chaotic life is better when it's shared with a partner. And I'll go to the kitchen and take Riley's phone from her."

Yvonne walked to her car, then drove to Johns Hopkins, trying to still the butterflies in her stomach and hoping that this time her Pop Pop was right. She didn't want to barge in on his family at such a stressful time if her presence there was an imposition, if Leo truly didn't want her there.

Her phone rang when she was halfway to the hospital.

"Hello?"

"Yvonne, it's Sunnie."

"Hey, listen, this really isn't a good ti—"

"I picked up an extra shift at the hospital tonight because quite a few nurses are out with a stomach bug. People are puking left and right around here."

"Lovely," Yvonne murmured. "Thanks for sharing."

Her cousin, Sunnie, was a nurse at Johns Hopkins. Though she typically worked in the oncology unit, Yvonne knew she pitched in wherever and whenever needed.

"That's not why I called. Leo's here. His dad had a heart attack."

"I know," Yvonne said. "I'm on my way, unless you thi—"

"Excellent," Sunnie responded, before Yvonne could ask if her cousin thought that was a good idea. "Leo doesn't look right."

"What do you mean?"

"He's...I don't know. He's always struck me as the steady-as-a-rock type, but he looks pretty shaken up right now."

"How is his dad?"

"They're still running tests."

"Okay. I'll be there in a few minutes."

Yvonne broke a few speed limits to get there quicker. She parked her car, then walked into the emergency room.

She spotted Leo, his mom, sister and brother sitting in a quiet corner of the waiting room before they saw her. Then, as if he sensed she was there, Leo looked up, his gaze meeting hers.

She hesitated, but Leo didn't.

He was across the waiting room in less than five seconds, and then, she was in his arms. He hugged her tight. "I'm so glad you're here," he whispered, his lips next to her ear.

"I was worried," she said, her voice muffled, her face pressed against his chest. Leo wasn't letting go. And neither was she. "About your dad."

And you, she thought.

They stood there for a minute, Leo clinging tightly to her. She started to pull away once, but his grip firmed up, so she held on longer. She would stay there as long as he needed her.

Finally, he released her. "I really am glad you're here. I..."

"You what?"

He frowned. "I thought I was going to lose it there for a minute. I was barely holding on by a thread, and then you walked in." She could tell he took no pleasure in admitting that.

"Are you okay now?"

He nodded. "Yeah. I...uh...the way I left your place, and then coming here, my dad..."

His words were a jumbled mess, but she could follow his line of thought just fine. "How is he?"

Leo shook his head and shrugged. "They're not telling us anything. When I first got here, I went in and saw him. He looked gray and they had a bunch of wires hooked up to him. I'm not used to seeing my dad look so...weak."

She'd just had a similar thought about Pop Pop.

"Then the doctor shooed us out so they could run some tests."

"He's in good hands, Leo. This hospital is the best. They'll figure out what's wrong and fix it. And Sunnie's working a shift tonight. I'll find her and see if she can come tell you what's going on."

Leo nodded, but when she started to walk away, he tugged her into his arms again for another quick hug. "Thanks for coming, Vonnie."

"All you ever have to do is ask."

One of his lips curled upwards. "Ask for help. If I'm not mistaken, *that* might have actually been your first advice to me."

Yvonne laughed softly. "I'll be sure to add it to the list when I get home."

"There's a list?"

"There will be when I get home. I'm losing track. Told you that you were a tough case."

He laughed, and she soaked in the sound of it.

Unfortunately, it was short-lived. "Listen, Vonnie, about earlier—"

She placed her finger over his lips. "No. There will be time to talk about that later. Right now, we focus on your dad. Okay?"

"Will you at least let me apologize?"

She grinned and shook her head. "Not necessary."

"Of course it is."

"No. It really isn't. Let me see if I can track Sunnie down while you go sit with your mom. It looks like she needs you."

One mention of his mom seemed to do the trick, as shaken Leo vanished, replaced instead by the strong, take-charge man she'd loved half her life.

She watched as he walked over and sat next to his mom, wrapping his arm around her shoulders as she leaned into him, fighting back worried tears.

Yvonne headed for the nurse's station, grateful that she'd come.

She was going to help Leo through the next few hours...and then, she was going to share the biggest secret to a happy life with him.

Love conquers all.

Leo followed Yvonne home from the hospital. It was so late it was early, and he didn't want her driving home, then walking into the pub alone in the wee hours of morning.

They'd run an entire battery of tests on his dad and confirmed that he had indeed had a heart attack. Apparently, he'd been experiencing symptoms all day but hadn't said anything. While they planned to run more tests tomorrow, the doctor felt certain bypass surgery would be necessary. Something that was risky, given the fact he was a diabetic.

It sounded like his dad was facing a long road to recovery, one that wouldn't be easy.

Josh had pulled Leo aside as they were leaving the hospital to suggest that he consider moving home until their dad was on his feet. Leo said he'd think about it, but reminded Josh it wasn't just himself he would be uprooting. Vince was halfway through middle school, a treacherous time if there ever was one. The kid was already struggling in his classes. Leo feared what would happen if he yanked his son out of a school where he had loads of friends—and apparently, a girlfriend—into one where he didn't know anyone.

Leo had been the new kid once. He recalled how scary that

first month or so was, and he'd been lucky and found the Collins cousins early, so he hadn't been totally alone.

Once they arrived, he parked his truck and got out.

"You don't have to walk me to the door," Yvonne said, meeting him halfway. Then she looked at him more closely.

God only knew what she saw. He was strung out and exhausted. Nervous energy and weariness.

"Leo," she said, cupping his face with her hands. "Are you okay to drive home?"

One look at her face and every shitty, horrible thought flew out of his head. "I'm not going home."

She gave him a tired grin. "Ever or just tonight? You're not considering that monastery route again, are you?"

He grasped her hand and pulled her toward the back door of the pub. She unlocked the door, their way lit by dim nightlights along the corridor by the storeroom. They'd enter the pub from that direction and then head upstairs.

Actually, they wouldn't.

He couldn't make it that far.

Leo used his grip on her hand to stop her halfway down the hallway, then pushed her against the wall.

Yvonne's hands flew to his shoulders and she lifted her face as he took her lips in a hungry, brutal kiss.

He wasted no time unfastening her jeans and pulling them down. Yvonne never blinked twice, didn't offer a bit of resistance. Instead, she kicked them off when they hit her ankles. Apparently, his unbridled haste was contagious.

Yvonne gave up on the kisses, glancing down to unbutton and unzip his jeans. Within seconds, her hand was there, drawing his erection out, her fist wrapped around him tightly.

She was giving him exactly what he needed, even after he'd left her hanging earlier. That thought had him moving faster. He wasn't stopping this time.

"Pill?" he asked.

She nodded.

He lifted one of her legs, her knee tucked over his arm, and drove his cock home in one hard, rough thrust.

Yvonne's head flew back, banging against the wall, but Leo couldn't stop, couldn't slow down. She was so hot...so wet. He slammed inside her, thrust after thrust, the wall at her back and his grip on her leg the only thing holding her upright. His free hand cupped the nape of her neck and he leaned toward her, stealing a quick kiss.

Yvonne nipped at his lower lip, the sting driving his arousal higher.

"Harder," she cried, her hands digging into his upper arms. With only one foot on the floor, on tiptoe, she was clearly seeking purchase. He'd be sporting bruises on his arms tomorrow, but he didn't care. Chances were good he was leaving a few on her as well.

"God, Leo. Fuck me. Fuck me harder!"

He increased his speed, the two of them coming at each other like unchained beasts. Yvonne leaned forward and sank her teeth into his pec through his shirt. She was a biter. He liked it. Liked knowing that she was as insane as him, out of control, wild.

Three more thrusts and she came, loudly. Crying out his name as well as a string of curses that would have made her aunt Riley proud.

Leo slowed his movements but didn't stop. He loved the way her pussy clenched against his dick. Earlier, he'd wanted to come with her the first time.

He didn't want that anymore.

Once her orgasm began to wane, he slid out, twisting her until she faced the wall, tugging her ass toward him.

"Put your hands on the wall and hold on, baby."

Yvonne had only just managed to lift her hands when he slammed back inside her from behind. He was buried to the hilt, his cock filling her completely. He held still for a split second, just long enough for her to feel how deep he was. Then he started moving again, plowing into her with the same speed, the same force.

He'd never fucked a woman this hard. In his right mind, he would have found the strength to rein himself in, would have taken more care.

"Fuck me like you mean it," Yvonne goaded. "God, Leo... I need you. Need you so bad."

His fingers tightened on her hips. Fuck control. He'd spent a lifetime holding on to it, fearing the day he'd finally lose it.

There was nothing scary here.

"Bend over more. Grip your ankles."

Yvonne pushed away from the wall and did as he said, groaning as his cock slid a millimeter deeper, his cock touching her in places he doubted she'd ever been touched before. Without her hands on the wall, the only thing keeping her in place was him. With each forward thrust, he used his grip to pull her ass against him. She was completely at his mercy. Completely his.

A dozen more strokes and she was there again. He felt her legs begin to give way as she trembled with her second orgasm, this one stronger than the first.

Slowly, he guided them to the floor, his cock still buried to the hilt. He managed to get her to her hands and knees, gritting his teeth to keep his own climax at bay as her inner muscles pulsed and throbbed against his erection.

"I'm not done with you yet."

Yvonne lowered her upper body, supporting herself with her elbows rather than her hands.

She looked over her shoulder at him and shook her head. "No."

For a split second, he panicked.

Until she said, "I'm not done with *you*."

Fuck.

Before he could consider that, she took over, pressing her ass back, driving his cock inside deeper before retreating, then doing it again.

Leo knelt there, watching as she fucked herself on his dick. Her smooth pale ass moving, moving, moving.

He lifted his hand and slapped it.

Yvonne's pussy muscles twitched and she groaned.

He did it again. And again. The cheeks of her ass flushed pink, then red, but he didn't stop. He couldn't.

Yvonne was out of her mind, moving against him like a woman possessed, capable of speaking only one word, over and over.

"More!"

Leo's balls constricted. He'd run out of time. Reaching for her, he gripped her hair, closing his fist and using it to tug her upright, until he could wrap his other arm around her, his free hand finding her right breast, cupping it.

He pistoned his hips inside her a half-dozen times more and then…oblivion.

"Fuck. *Fuck*. God, Vonnie. Baby!"

It took him a few seconds before he realized she was coming again too. Her entire body shook in his arms, so he tightened his grip as he came inside her, filling her.

It was the first time he'd ever consciously taken a woman without a condom. He'd even worn one the night Denise got pregnant with Vince, though the thing had broken, and because he'd been young and stupid and inexperienced, he hadn't even realized.

This time, he knew exactly what he was doing.

They remained there, kneeling together on the floor for several minutes, neither of them speaking. Given the loudness of their breathing, he suspected she was no more capable of speech than he was.

Finally, she blew out a long sigh, her body relaxed in his arms, and her head fell backwards onto his shoulder. She turned her face to him, kissing him on the jaw. "So...how 'bout those Orioles? Think we've got a chance at the pennant this year?"

Leo laughed, and then he laughed some more, his whole body shaking as he tried to get himself under control. It was no use as tears started to stream down his cheeks. "There is something seriously wrong with you," he said, trying to catch his breath again, though this time for a different reason.

Yvonne gave him a delighted grin as she crawled away from him, reaching for her jeans.

He stood up, then offered her a hand to help her rise as well. She was unsteady, and Leo waited for the first twinge of guilt to appear. He had been way too rough.

Incredibly, there was no guilt. Or regret. Or anxiety.

Only joy.

He helped her pull her jeans back on, then he hitched his back up over his hips, zipping and buttoning them. Apart from that, the rest of their clothing had remained in place.

Leo reached around her, gripping her ass cheek and squeezing a little, getting a kick out of her slight wince, then the narrowing of her eyes.

"Proud of that, aren't you?" she asked.

He nodded, grinning unrepentantly. "You're going to think about me every time you sit down the next couple of days."

She gave him a sexy wink. "I'm going to think about you sitting or standing. That was the best sex I've ever had."

Leo snorted. "I took you in the back hallway of the pub, Vonnie. Not my most romantic move."

"Romance is overrated."

He'd met his soul mate.

"But," she said, "we better move this party upstairs to my bedroom. Riley will be here in an hour or so to start getting ready for the breakfast crowd."

He followed her upstairs. The apartment was still dark, except for the dim illumination from the streetlamps outside. Once they were in her room, he closed and locked the door.

Yvonne was already taking her clothes off, so he followed suit, amazed at how natural it already felt to be naked in front of her. Everything that had happened between them today was new, yet at the same time, not.

There was a lot to be said for that old "friends make the best lovers" adage.

Naked, Yvonne crawled beneath the covers, then patted the bed next to her. "You should try to get a few hours' sleep. I suspect tomorrow will be a busy day for you."

He nodded, climbing into the bed next to her. Yvonne twisted away from him so that he could spoon her from behind. Downstairs, he'd taken her with very little touching or kissing or even looking, as they'd remained fairly clothed.

Leo would have expected to fall asleep instantly, but now that he had her naked body pressed against his, he felt rejuvenated and anxious to discover more of her secrets. His fingers traveled over her soft skin, tracing lines around her breasts and her nipples as he lightly kissed the side of her neck.

Yvonne mewed like a well-loved kitten, wiggling her ass against his cock, which was slowly starting to thicken.

Reaching back, Yvonne did her own awkward exploration, her hands stroking his hips before moving along his ass.

After playing with her breasts for several minutes, Leo decided to investigate the territory due south. He brushed his fingertips through the hair of her pussy, then pressed deeper, finding her clit.

Yvonne sucked in a soft breath, pushing her ass more fully against his erection.

They continued to tease each other, Leo caressing her clit as she rubbed her ass against him as the minutes ticked by and the first light of dawn cut through the darkness.

"Turn around," he said, his voice suddenly gruffer.

Yvonne rolled to her back and he leaned down to kiss her. Unlike the outright attack downstairs, this touch was gentle, softer. Her lips parted and their tongues touched. He cupped her cheek as they kissed, while her hands found their way to his chest.

"I can't get enough of you," he murmured when they parted briefly for air.

She smiled. "I'm not complaining."

Leo shifted until he was over her, Yvonne's legs parting for him. He ran his finger along her slit, concerned about taking her again so soon after everything they'd just done.

She was wet and ready, so he placed the head of his cock inside and slid home slowly. Neither of them was in a hurry to rush to the end, time meaningless as they simply lay there, locked together, looking into each other's eyes.

Yvonne lifted her legs, wrapping her ankles around his waist as he gently rocked in and out. He wanted to prove to her he could give her anything she needed. A rough, hard fuck or soft lovemaking.

Anything. He'd give her *anything*.

They kissed as he moved inside her, Yvonne lifting her hips on each return to take him deeper.

The sun had just burst through the curtains when she whispered, "Leo. I'm…"

"Me too."

They came together, a quieter melding of two bodies, though no less passionate, no less powerful.

It was on the tip of Leo's tongue to tell her loved her when his phone pinged.

Reality always found a way to crash in on him at just the wrong time.

Yvonne gave him an understanding smile. "You better see who that is."

He nodded as he withdrew, sitting up slowly before grabbing his jeans off the floor to fish his phone out of his pocket.

It was a message from his mother, telling him they'd scheduled his dad for more testing at nine o'clock and asking if he could be there.

It was just after six now, and he still needed to head home, shower, change clothes and figure out what to do with the boys if Ryder couldn't take the day off. Looked like he wasn't getting any sleep today.

Glancing over his shoulder at Yvonne, her hair a tangled, sexy mess on the pillow, wiped away any regret he had about that. Losing a night's sleep to be with her was worth it.

He texted his mom and said he'd be there at nine. Then placed his phone on the nightstand.

"I can't stay," he said, bending down to kiss her.

"I know."

His phone pinged again. "You have a hammer? I think I know a way to stop that annoying sound."

She giggled as he grabbed his phone once more.

This text was from Josh, who'd obviously gotten the same message from their mother. His brother and sister had elected to remain on the farm today, and they needed Leo to head out there after their dad's tests to pack up a few orders and run a couple deliveries. Then Josh told him to bring Vince along, that they needed an extra pair of hands to help bring in some crops.

Leo bristled at the suggestion. While he saw nothing wrong with Vince helping out and learning the ways of farming, he refused to make his twelve-year-old son a workhorse the same way his father had Leo and his siblings. He'd promised himself that Vince would have a real childhood, complete with friends, after-school activities and hands that weren't perpetually calloused.

The problem was, it had always been an issue of pride for his dad that the family farm had been maintained strictly by Watsons since they'd bought the land four generations earlier. They hired hands to help during the busy season, but the bulk of the work had always been done by them.

While his mom and sister ran the farm stand, he, Josh, and Dad planted the crops, then tended and harvested them. When Denise died, Leo wasn't able to do as much of the actual farm work, losing too much time commuting to the city, so he took the deliveries over from his grandfather, who had passed away the previous year from cancer.

When he was younger, Leo had discovered ways they could do more with the land that had been passed down through the generations in the Watson family. In the last decade, they'd bought chickens so they could sell eggs, planted apple trees and added a pumpkin patch. During the fall, they did hayrides. They were ideally located just forty-five minutes outside the city, so they were a pretty popular field trip location for the city elementary schools.

Leo had insisted on more than one occasion that it was time to hire more full-time help for the actual farm work, so they could expand those other aspects of the family business. Unfortunately, neither Josh nor his dad would entertain the notion, which meant they all pulled longer hours in the field.

"Everything okay?" Yvonne asked, when he'd stared at his phone in silence too long.

"Yeah. Just thinking about how..." He started to feel groggy, the lack of sleep catching up with him.

"I know you're tired, so I'll give you a bye. Please refer back to that first piece of advice."

He looked at her for a second before a light went on.

Ask for help.

He grimaced. "Yvonne, I can't keep—"

"Holy shit," she said, sitting up. "If you finish that sentence, I swear to God I'll punch you in the nose."

He chuckled. "You spend too much time with those wild cousins of yours. It's made you violent."

Yvonne wasn't distracted or dissuaded. "What do you need me to do?"

She hadn't gotten any sleep either. And none of these problems were hers.

"Do you have work today?" he asked.

She nodded. "Yes, but I can—"

"I've learned my lesson, Vonnie. But you aren't the one I'm asking for help. Not this time." He texted Josh and said he'd get to the farm as soon as he could. Then he called Ryder. It was early, but fuck it.

"Hello." Ryder cleared his throat. It was obvious Leo had woken him. "Leo?"

"Sorry to call you so early, man."

"No, no." He could tell Ryder was trying to shake himself awake. "That's no problem. How's your dad?"

"They're doing some more tests at nine and then I need to run out to the farm to take care of stuff there. I'm going to be home in a little while to shower and change, but I was wondering if—"

"You don't even have to ask. I'll take the day off and man the fort. Shit, it's the least I can do. You've been covering for me for weeks. You take care of your dad and I'll handle things here."

"Thanks, Ryder."

"I'll see you when you get here."

They hung up and Leo felt the tension in his shoulders relax.

"Everything good?"

He nodded. "Ryder's going to take care of the boys today."

She smiled. "That wasn't so hard, was it?"

Old Leo, the friend, would have given her some sort of smart-ass reply to tease her for being so cocky.

New Leo couldn't summon anything more than gratitude. He kissed her. "You're brilliant, amazing, the smartest person I know."

It looked like the old friend part of Yvonne was struggling with new Leo. She gave him a suspicious expression, clearly waiting for the punchline. When it didn't come, she flushed slightly, and he could tell she was touched by his kind words.

Of course, old or new, Yvonne could never pass up the chance for a joke. "Are you sure I still can't convince you to put some of that in writing? You have no idea how handy something like that would be around here."

"I'll consider it." Leo sighed. "I guess I should get dressed and head home for a little while."

She nodded. "Yeah. Okay."

He didn't stand up. Couldn't leave her so soon, not after the night they'd just shared. He glanced down when she ran her fingers over his upper arm, tracing his tattoo. He could just about make out a faint bruise beneath the ink.

"Lay down, Vonnie."

She did as he asked, though he could see she was surprised by—and curious about—the request.

She was partially covered by the sheet, so he tugged it down, baring her completely. Then he ran his eyes—and hands—over her, memories of how roughly he'd taken her downstairs niggling at his conscience.

Yvonne didn't mistake his actions as foreplay, her eyes narrowing slightly when he told her to roll over to her stomach.

"I'm fine," she said, not moving.

"I'd like to see that for myself. I was pretty rough with you."

"God, you're not going to start apologizing, are you?"

He shook his head. "Nope. Because I'm not sorry."

"Good. Wait!" she said, as her eyes filled with horror. "You're not going to promise not to do it again, are you?"

"I don't make promises I can't keep."

She let loose with a long, loud sigh of relief, then she did as he asked, rolling to her stomach. She gave a little mewl of pleasure as he ran his hands softly over her slightly pink ass cheeks. There were some faint red marks on her back that he assumed had been left when he took her against the wall.

"You sure you're okay?" The gentleman in him couldn't stop from asking the question, even as the too-dominant lover reveled in knowing she'd feel the effects of their lovemaking all day long.

"I'm better than okay."

"I'm afraid I lost control with you."

She shook her head. "No. You didn't. There's a difference between losing control and letting go."

He'd already discovered that for himself last night.

"And if you didn't have to leave, I'd push you to your back, sink down on that thick, hard cock of yours and ride you until I convinced you to let go again."

"Dirty talk," he murmured, leaning over her to place a kiss in the center of her back. "Just when I thought you couldn't get any sexier."

She shivered when he traced her spine with his tongue, traveling downwards until he reached the line between her ass cheeks.

"I don't mean to brag, but I'm pretty good at dirty talk too," he murmured, nipping her ass.

"Prove it," she whispered.

"Next time we're together, I'm going to bend you over this bed and finger fuck that tight little asshole of yours. Then I'm going to push you to the edge of an orgasm and make you beg for hours on end before I finally take you from behind and let you come."

"God," Yvonne said, the word all breath, no sound. "You win."

He chuckled, then regretfully forced himself to push away from her. "I hate leaving you."

She flopped to her back. While he was fighting hard to rally, she was losing her fight to sleep. "I'll text you later."

"Okay." He kissed her on the cheek, then stood and got dressed. "Get some rest, baby."

"Mmmm." Her eyes were already closed, her speech slowing when she said, "I'm going to have very sweet dreams."

❧ 8 ❧

"Hey, Vonnie. We're going to the fair!"

Yvonne turned around at the sound of Clint's voice. She managed to brace herself mere seconds before the sweet little boy launched himself into her arms. "The fair? No way! I love the fair."

"Good. You're coming with us."

She glanced up at the sound of Leo's voice and found him just inside the entrance to Sunday's Side, standing next to Vince. Both of them were smiling at her.

It had been two days since she'd seen Leo, though they'd texted quite a lot. Actually, last night, it was more accurate to say they'd sexted...and it was fucking hot.

"To the fair?"

Leo nodded, and she could see he was a hell of a lot less excited about it than Clint. "My folks promised to take the boys, but...well...Dad's bypass surgery is scheduled for the day after tomorrow and Mom insisted that I take the boys instead. She hated disappointing them. They've been looking forward to it all summer."

"Can you come with us?" Vince asked hopefully.

"Weeellllll…" Yvonne looked around the restaurant and spotted her dad talking to two customers, then she turned back to Vince and gave him a wink. "Let me see if the boss will give me the afternoon off."

Vince grinned. "That's your dad."

She crooked her finger at him. "Yeah, but he's one tough customer. Come with me. If he sees I've got a hot date, he'll never be able to say no to me."

Vince laughed but followed her across the restaurant.

Her father saw them approaching, smiling when he saw Vince. "Hey, Vince. Long time no see." He glanced behind them, waving to Leo and Clint. "What are you guys up to?"

"We're going to the fair, and we wanted to know if Vonnie could come with us."

Yvonne hated leaving her dad shy one waitress on short notice, but so far today, business had been damn slow.

"I think that would be fine. If we get in a pinch, I'll call around and see if one of the other waitresses can come in for a few hours."

Yvonne kissed her dad on the cheek. "Thanks, Dad."

"Have a good time, Vonnie."

She took off her apron, then excused herself to run upstairs to grab her purse and sunglasses while the guys waited for her in the pub, chatting with Padraig.

"Ready," she said, when she joined them again.

Leo held the door to the pub open for all of them to leave but didn't reach for her hand. She suspected he was playing it cool in front of the boys. They hadn't discussed what they'd say to Vince about what was going on between them.

Of course, they hadn't talked much at all beyond what sexual positions they were going to try the next time they managed to steal five minutes alone.

Leo opened the passenger door of his truck and helped her in while the boys clamored into the backseat.

Leo crossed to the driver's side and fired up the engine. His old Ford F150 had seen better days, but according to Leo, it still "did the trick." They drove to the Maryland State Fair with the windows down, country music blasting on the radio, grinning like fools as they chatted about all the fair food they were going to eat.

The boys were determined to try fried Oreos, Yvonne was looking forward to her funnel cake. Leo told them they could gorge themselves on the desserts if they wanted, but he was getting a jumbo Italian sausage with the works.

Once they arrived, Vince and Clint immediately dragged them to the stand to buy tickets for rides. Leo plopped down a twenty, and then he and Yvonne followed them to the Tilt-A-Whirl.

"Wanna give it a spin?" Leo asked.

Yvonne shook her head. "No thanks. Me and spinning in fast circles do not agree. I have a date with a funnel cake that I'd like to keep."

They waved when the boys got on the ride. Once the ride started spinning, Leo slid his arm around her waist and pulled her toward him for a kiss that was probably skirting the boundaries of "fair appropriate."

"God," he murmured against her lips. "I've been waiting to do that for days."

She grinned. "I admire your restraint in front of the boys. And...my dad."

"Guess we need to figure out what we're telling people about us," he mused.

"What do you *want* to tell them?"

Leo's hand slid from her waist to her ass for just a split second, giving it a playful squeeze. "I want to tell everyone you're mine, but..."

Leo glanced toward the ride once more. It was starting to slow down, which meant there were two very dizzy little boys about to head in their direction.

"But there's no rush," Yvonne said. "We've only just crossed the line from friends to lovers. Let's keep it to ourselves for a little while. Just to be sure."

"Sure of what?"

Yvonne shrugged. "I guess that it'll stick."

His eyes narrowed slightly. "You think it won't?"

"I've wanted this since I was fourteen, and if it was up to me, I'd start carving our names into every tree on the planet, then I'd skywrite it for good measure. But..." She crinkled her nose. "I think we have to do that silly adulting thing, take things slow because if it doesn't work out..."

She didn't want to finish that sentence because her heart didn't want to consider this wasn't forever, but Kelli's words about her possibly hurting more than just Leo kept coming back to her.

"If it doesn't work out, there's more than just you and me getting hurt."

She wanted to ask Leo if he'd ever talked to Vince about the future, about the possibility that Leo may start dating and even get married, but there wasn't time. Vince was already off the ride—unsteady on his feet, but grinning from ear to ear. He helped Clint down, then the two of them raced back to Leo and Yvonne.

"I don't know where they find the energy," Leo said.

"Can we play some games?" Clint asked.

"Sure." The four of them meandered through the tents, trying to decide which to play. Actually, she and Leo were looking at the games. Clint and Vince were eyeballing the prizes, trying to decide which ones they wanted to win.

Yvonne pulled up short when they reached the Strong Man game.

"Want to test your strength?" Leo asked her.

"Nope. Want to test *yours*."

Leo shook his head and started to walk on, but Vince and Clint blocked his path.

"Do it!" Vince urged.

"Why don't *you* give it a try?" Leo asked his son.

Vince shook his head. "I'm not as strong as you. I bet you could ring that bell."

There were several other young men in the line ahead of them, and so far none of them had managed to strike hard enough to win.

"I'll buy your Italian sausage if you do," Yvonne said, adding more incentive.

Leo considered that. "I want the works, remember?"

She laughed. "You haven't rung the bell yet."

They got in line, watching as two more men failed to win.

"Thing is probably rigged," Leo muttered.

The moment Leo said that, the man just before them struck hard enough to ring the bell.

"There goes that excuse," Yvonne teased.

"I'm going to make you pay for this later," he whispered in her ear.

"I'm looking forward to it," she threw back with a sultry wink.

From the suddenly hungry look on Leo's face, she knew her taunt had been effective, and she wondered if she'd catch a glimpse of anything bulging in his pants if she snuck a look below his belt.

The guy running the booth called Leo up and he took the mallet.

"Go, Dad!" Vince called out as Clint bounced up and down on his toes excitedly.

Yvonne had definitely had an ulterior motive when she'd suggested this game. As Leo threw the mallet back, she got a peek at his muscular arms bulging beneath his T-shirt. One of these days she was going to run her tongue along every single line of the tattoos that painted both of his upper arms.

Leo swung hard and rang the bell.

She, Vince and Clint cheered as the man asked Leo what prize he wanted. Leo pointed to Yvonne. "Ask her."

Yvonne glanced at the large array of stuffed animals, then consulted with Clint. "Which one do you think I should get?"

"The Pokémon!" he shouted.

She selected the Pokémon—Pikachu, to be exact—then thanked Clint, who gallantly offered to carry it for her.

"Come on," Leo said. "Somebody owes me a sausage."

They ate their fair food as they walked along the lines of arts and crafts and canned goods on display, but that foray was brief, the boys too impatient to return to "the fun stuff."

"Let's do more rides," Vince said.

Leo led them back to the rides, and he and Yvonne snuck kisses as the boys rode the Swing Ride and the Orbiter.

"Okay," Leo said when they returned. "Four tickets left. What should it be?"

Both boys were looking a bit green after the last ride, so Yvonne wasn't surprised when they elected for something a little tamer.

"What about the Ferris wheel?" Vince suggested. "You and Vonnie can ride on that one too."

"Sounds like fun," Yvonne said. "Clint and I can—"

"You and Leo should ride together," Clint said. "I'll ride with Vince."

Yvonne tried to sneak a peek at Vince's face to see what he thought of that suggestion, but he didn't appear to be listening, his attention snagged by three girls about his age who were walking by.

She'd told Leo he didn't have to worry about Vince's hormones until high school, but she was suddenly revising that opinion.

"What do you say, Vonnie? You and me?" Leo asked.

Yvonne nodded and the four of them got in line. The boys climbed in first, then they got into the car directly behind them.

As the Ferris wheel began spinning, Leo slipped his hand along the back of their seat, drawing his fingers over the nape of her neck.

She sighed contentedly. "I can't thank you enough for inviting me along today. This brings back so many great memories. My family never missed the fair when I was a kid."

"Funny. I was just sitting here thinking eighteen was too old for my first visit. It's definitely more exciting when you're a kid."

Yvonne twisted to look at him. "You're kidding, right?"

Leo shook his head. "My family subscribes to that saying, 'All work and no play.'"

Yvonne waited for him to finish, but he didn't. "You realize there's more to that saying, right?"

"Not in my family."

"The fair feels like something you would do. Aren't there contests for vegetables and canning and stuff like that?"

"If we'd come to the fair, we would have had to close the stand. My dad never closes the stand. Always said that was what fed us and kept a roof over our heads."

"I thought it was your parents who'd promised to bring the boys."

Leo laughed. "There's a big difference between parents and grandparents."

"I get that."

"I think I'm always giving the wrong impression of my parents. It wasn't like we begged to come to the fair and they said no. We were homeschooled, so there weren't other kids telling us about the rides or the cotton candy or stuff. I didn't realize how cool it was until I started school. I think it was you, actually, who turned my head. You brought me a candy apple on the first day of school my senior year, said you'd gotten it here, then you proceeded to tell me about the games and the rides. I came with Lochlan for the first time, the summer after we graduated. He was trying to cheer me up about my breakup with Denise."

"Did it work?"

Leo rolled his eyes. "You know me, Vonnie. I've always been a miserable bastard."

She bent toward him and kissed him on the cheek. "If that were true, I wouldn't be on this Ferris wheel with you."

"I guess all I'm saying is, there wasn't anything horrible about my childhood. My parents loved us, but no one could accuse them of spoiling us. I've watched them with Vince, and I think maybe they realize there was too much work and not enough fun when we were growing up. They're mellowing a little with age." He sighed. "Now if only Josh would."

Leo was the baby of his family, and there was a fairly large age gap between him and his siblings. His sister, Marie, was ten years older than him, his brother, Josh, five. He'd admitted once that his sister had always felt more like a second mom.

"Fruit didn't fall far from the tree with your brother, I'm afraid." Yvonne had been around Josh enough to know the man had zero sense of humor and even fewer people skills. He was gruff, judgmental, and pretty unforgiving.

Leo shrugged. "I'm afraid nothing I've ever done has been good enough for Josh. At least I figured that out a long time ago, so I stopped letting it hurt me."

"I guess I was lucky. Only child. And super spoiled."

Leo wrapped the arm resting on the back of the seat around her shoulders and pulled her close, placing a kiss on the side of her head. "You can say that spoiled thing again."

She punched him lightly in the stomach.

"Dad's surgery is day after tomorrow."

"I know."

"So I'm not sure when I'll see you again. My time will be split between the hospital and the farm and the boys. Ryder seems to think he'll be home more often, now that the training for his new job is just about finished."

"It's okay, Leo. I know things are crazy right now."

He blew out a long breath. "Things are always crazy."

She didn't know how to respond to that. It was one of the reasons he'd given her at the beginning for not wanting to embark on a relationship. She could hardly fault him now for being busy. Not that she would.

It was just...she could see him every single minute of every single day and it still wouldn't be enough. He consumed her thoughts during the day and her dreams at night. But telling him that would only add to his stress and his feeling of letting down someone he cared about. So she held her tongue.

"Come back to the house with us. I'll drive you home later after Ryder gets back from work."

She nodded. "Okay."

"I can't get enough of you," he admitted.

She laughed. "Get out of my head. I was just thinking the same thing, but I didn't want to make you feel bad. Your family needs you."

"You don't have to shield your feelings with me, Vonnie. God knows you never have in the past."

The ride began to slow down, stopping every few feet as people got off and others got on.

The sun was hanging low in the sky, dusk approaching. While she was delighted to get to spend more time with Leo, it was going to be a long evening of keeping her distance around the boys.

With that thought in mind, she stole one more kiss, intending to keep it quick. Once again, she and Leo seemed to be in synch. Except he wasn't satisfied with her fast peck. When she started to pull away, he gripped the back of her neck and kissed her again, this one long and deep and definitely *not* fair appropriate.

They parted when the Ferris wheel stopped again, the boys hopping off.

She caught a glimpse of Vince looking at them. She couldn't tell if he'd witnessed the kiss or not, but he wasn't smiling. In fact, he looked upset.

She glanced at Leo, who was looking in Vince's direction and frowning as well.

Shit.

❦ *9* ❦

When they were all together again, they headed for the truck. The ride home was quieter than the journey to the fair, all of them full and hot and tired. Even the music from the radio seemed worn out, as one slow country ballad after another played. Yvonne snuck several peeks back at Vince, who looked out the window during the entire trip.

"You forgot to take Vonnie home," Clint said as they pulled into the driveway to their house.

"She's going to hang out at our place a little while," Leo explained.

Clint brightened. "Cool."

At least one of the boys seemed happy to have her around. Vince didn't say anything. Instead, he opened the back door of the truck and climbed out without looking at her.

Leo gave her a smile she assumed was meant to be comforting, but it didn't help much. Leo said Vince had been grumpy of late, and he was blaming puberty. Maybe that was it.

They walked into the house together, Boomer waiting for them at the door. "You guys go on back and get your showers now. Wash off the sweat and fair dirt. Then we can put a movie in until bedtime."

Clint and Vince were obviously tired because neither boy put up a fuss about having to shower. She dropped down on the couch as Leo wandered to the kitchen, then returned with two beers—a PBR for him, a Corona for her—and joined her.

Yvonne glanced toward the entrance of the living room, wondering if she dared to chance another kiss.

"Clint is the quickest showerer in the east," Leo said, in answer to her unspoken desire. "He'll be back here in less than five minutes."

"He's a bit like a Tasmanian Devil, isn't he? Always whirling around."

Leo gave her a look she couldn't read until he said, "That's the pot calling the kettle black."

"I have no idea what you mean," she protested.

Leo leaned toward her, close enough she could feel his breath on her cheek. "Don't worry, Vonnie. I like the way you're in constant motion. Especially the way you squirm around when I put my mouth on your cl—"

"Vonnie!" Vince called her name from down the hallway. Just when Leo was getting to the good part.

"Hold that thought," she said, rising from the couch.

Leo stood and followed her, and she smiled when she noticed him adjusting the front of his jeans.

He narrowed his eyes at her knowing grin. "My permanent state when you're around," he grumbled.

"I totally get it. I'm hot," she joked.

He smacked her ass, chuckling as they walked toward the boy's bedroom.

Vince was standing just inside the doorway. He pointed toward Clint's bed, where the little boy was lying down.

"My stomach hurts," Clint said, clutching his middle.

"Oh no." Yvonne made her way to the side of his bed. "I was afraid of this. You ate way too much junk at the fair." She placed her hand on his forehead to see if he was feverish. "Cool as a cucumber," she said, relieved it didn't appear to be that stomach bug Sunnie mentioned going around earlier in the week.

"Can you stay with me and rub it until it stops hurting?" Clint groaned, the sound fifty-percent genuine, fifty-percent drama.

Yvonne glanced over just in time to see Leo rolling his eyes. She grinned. She'd babysat for Clint enough to know the boy was starving for motherly attention. In a house full of males, Clint's opportunities to be fussed over by a woman were few and far between. She and Darcy were always amused by his antics to garner their sympathy for all his "ailments," while also deeply grateful for the opportunity to nurture the motherless boy.

"Of course I will, baby. You lie right there on your back and let me rub it all better. I shouldn't have let you eat so much of that funnel cake. It was too greasy for your little tummy."

Clint gave her a weak smile, though there was no true pain in his expression.

"Do you think holding on to Pikachu might make you feel better?" she asked.

He nodded solemnly. "I think it would." The kid had true talent. He needed to move to Hollywood.

"I'll grab it from the living room," Leo said.

She'd carried the stuffed toy in from the truck, intending to give it to Clint anyway. He was probably skirting the line of too old for stuffed animals, but the way his face lit up when she took it from Leo and gave it to him proved he wasn't there yet.

"You still up for a movie, Vince?" Leo asked.

Vince shook his head. "No. I think I'll just watch TV in here. Okay?"

Leo nodded. "Sure. If that's what you want. Clint, you need anything? Water? Milk?"

Clint looked at Yvonne. "Would milk help my stomach?"

Sunnie was the nurse in the family. Yvonne didn't have a clue if it would help or not, but since she was now ninety-five percent sure he was faking, she nodded. "I think it would. Want me to get some for you?"

"Yes, please."

"How about you, Vince?" Yvonne asked over her shoulder. "Would you like some milk?"

Vince shook his head without looking at her. He was definitely in a fouler mood now than he had been before the Ferris wheel ride.

"What do you say, Vince?" Leo prompted.

"No, thank you," Vince grumbled.

Yvonne stood up. "I'll get the milk and be right back."

"I'll get it," Leo said.

"Can Vonnie get it for me?" Clint asked.

Leo opened his mouth, but Yvonne put her hand on his arm. "Some things require a woman's touch." She winked at him covertly, then the two of them left the room and headed to the kitchen.

"The kid's fine," Leo said, pulling a cup from the cabinet as she retrieved the milk from the refrigerator.

"I know. But he doesn't have a mother to fuss over him, and I think he misses it."

It was clear that hadn't occurred to Leo. "Oh. You think that's what it is? Clint and Vince don't really mention Denise much anymore. I'd started to wonder if they'd been too young when they lost her to really remember..."

"They haven't forgotten her, Leo. They never will." She poured the milk. "I'll run this back to Clint and meet you in the living room in a few minutes."

He nodded but didn't say anything else. She feared perhaps she'd upset him by mentioning Denise.

Wow. She was batting a thousand tonight...with the father *and* the son.

She comforted Clint for a few minutes more as he sipped his milk, but soon his stomach ache was forgotten as he and Vince become engrossed in *SpongeBob* repeats.

"I'm going to go watch a movie with Leo," she said, pressing a kiss to Clint's forehead.

"Okay, Vonnie. Night."

She turned, wondering if she should offer Vince the same good-night kiss, but he ignored her completely, his scowl firmly in place.

"Night, Vince," she said instead.

"Night."

She tried to still the uneasiness in her chest as she walked down the hallway and back to the living room. Ryder and Leo shared the three-bedroom, two-bathroom ranch Ryder and Denise had purchased shortly after their wedding. It was actually a fairly nice size, though she'd heard Ryder and Leo discussing the possibility of putting on an addition. Both men knew the day was coming when the boys would want their own rooms, plus Ryder was hoping for a larger home office and Leo was determined to get his own bathroom. As it was now, he shared one with Vince while Clint shared the other with Ryder. Leo thought the boys needed their own.

Fortunately, the house was situated on a large enough plot that they had more than enough room for the additions, and Leo had mentioned several months ago in passing that they had an architect drawing up the plans.

Leo was kicked back on the couch with Boomer when she entered.

"Boys settled?" he asked.

She nodded. "Yeah. I don't think they'll be awake much longer. They both look pretty worn out."

"It was a busy day for them. We spent a few hours working on the farm before heading into town to pick you up for the fair."

Leo turned on the TV, firing up an old *Mission Impossible* movie they'd both seen countless times before. His movie selection told her actually watching a movie was not part of his plan for the night.

She grinned when he reached for her hand and pulled her up. "What about the movie?"

"You want to watch it?"

She shook her head.

"Then come on."

Leo led her from the living room to his own bedroom, closing and locking the door behind them.

"What about the boys?" she asked.

"Sorry to say this is going to be a quiet quickie."

She laughed softly. "Pretty sure of yourself, aren't you, Mr. Watson?"

"You gotta have mercy on me, Vonnie. Three years was a long time to go without. The other night with you...I'm in pain, baby."

"Me too. Quiet quickie it is."

He reached for her, unfastening her jeans and helping her take them and her shoes off. He ran his hand over her breast, her shirt still in the way. He sighed regretfully. "Next time I get you in bed, we're going to be alone, naked and have all night."

"Not much of a challenge in that," she teased. They were speaking in hushed tones. While the boys' bedroom was at the far end of the hallway and the door was locked, neither of them was willing to risk discovery.

"Go to my bed and bend over, hands on the mattress."

If Yvonne hadn't already been soaking wet, his deep-voiced command would have done the trick.

He was right behind her, and by the time she was in position, his pants were already open, his erect cock in his hand.

With his free hand, he stroked her bare ass. "God, what I'd give to spank you right now."

She wiggled her ass at him suggestively, but he didn't take the bait.

"Too noisy. Especially the way you respond, all loud cries, screaming my name, begging for more," he whispered.

"I don't beg," she said, lying through her teeth.

He ran his finger along her slit, brushing her clit before sinking two fingers deep. "Is that right?"

She sighed blissfully, pushing her ass back against him on every inward thrust. Leo continued to stroke in and out, but he didn't add another finger, didn't increase his pace, didn't...

Ah. Of course. The asshole was waiting for her to beg.

She looked over her shoulder at him.

"Yes?" he said, with a shit-eating grin. "Did you want something?"

"It would serve you right if I gave you what you were asking for. Screamed your name. Loudly begged you to take me hard."

Leo narrowed his eyes, then glanced around the room.

A small groan escaped her when he pulled his fingers out and moved away. He returned with a clean shirt.

"Open your mouth."

She started to shake her head. "I was kidd—"

Leo stuffed some of the material into her mouth, then used the arms of the shirt to secure the makeshift gag.

She shook her head, not as a no, but as a way to see if she could dislodge it. She couldn't.

"Want me to take it out?" he asked.

She shook her head again. This time she meant no.

"You like it?"

Yvonne nodded. Leo was clearly into bondage, something she'd never really tried, but couldn't deny was a huge turn-on.

"You have no idea how sexy you are," he murmured.

He shifted to stand behind her once more, and she moaned —the sound muted by the shirt—as he slowly slid inside.

Even with the gag in, Yvonne tried to be quiet. She was fairly vocal in the bedroom, so forcing herself to remain silent was a new experience for her. As was the gag.

There was nothing about Leo that was predictable in the bedroom except the fact that he knew how to rev her engine. Fast or slow, deep or shallow, the man knew every button to push.

Right now, he was rocking inside her as gentle as a boat on a placid lake, one hand resting loosely on her hip as the other snuck around to caress her clit.

She arched her back, marveling at how close she was. Leo had said it would be a quickie. She'd interpreted that as something fast, something frantic, like the other night down in the pub. She never would have expected to be able to come so quickly like this.

Her head dropped to the mattress as she felt the swell of the wave, anticipating that sharp flash of almost-pain. Sex with Leo was seriously addictive.

She held her breath, and then—

Leo withdrew, his fingers falling away from her clit.

Her body was tense, but with nothing there to push her over...

She glanced over her shoulder, ready to blast him, but the gag prevented her complaints. Yvonne narrowed her eyes, but Leo merely chuckled.

"I know I said quickie," he murmured. "But that was *too* quick. You really need to exercise some restraint, baby."

Yvonne reached up, intent on pulling the gag from her mouth so she could give him an earful of exactly where he could stick his restraint. He grabbed her hands before she could accomplish that, drawing them behind her back.

Without her hands to hold her up, her head fell to the mattress. He applied just enough pressure to her caged wrists to keep her down.

Yvonne wasn't an innocent when it came to sex. She enjoyed it and she'd experimented plenty. However, she was starting to realize she was still a novice. Because great sex wasn't about all the positions, it was about experiencing it with a lover who knew how to pull out previously unseen desires.

Leo made love to her mind as much as her body, allowing her to explore things she never would have known to ask for.

Like this deep-seated desire to be held captive, helpless,

submissive. With anyone else, that would be terrifying, but with Leo—whom she trusted completely—it was mind-blowing, exciting, hugely arousing.

He held her wrists together with one of his calloused hands, letting her feel his strength, his power over her. With the other, he softly stroked her ass, petting her as gently as he would a newborn kitten.

So many contrasting feelings.

"That's better," he cooed, when she stopped trying to get up and instead relaxed, her body going limp. "Let's try this again. Are you going to come the second I slide back in?"

She shook her head. He wanted to draw this out, make it last. These stolen moments were so few and far between, she understood that need. They had to make every second count.

"Good. Because I want us to come together, Vonnie. Always together."

She nodded earnestly. She wanted the same, wanted him to know that, even though she couldn't say the words.

He released her hands, gripped his cock and guided it home once more. This time, he grasped her hips in a firm hold and fucked her the way she'd expected.

It was a hard, fast, explosive ride, one meant to test her. Yvonne fought back her orgasm for several minutes, the act of stopping herself a different sort of pleasurable pain, something she'd never felt before.

She was grateful for the gag in her mouth because she feared she'd never manage to keep herself from screaming when she finally did go over.

Leo, as always, seemed to know exactly what she was thinking. He bent over her, his chest pressed to her back, and whispered in her ear, "Not a sound, Yvonne. Not a single peep."

She slowly shook her head, her pussy clenching, her breath ragged. There was no way she'd succeed.

"I mean it," he murmured. "Not a sound."

She sucked in as much air as she could through her nose and the soft cotton filling her mouth, then closed her eyes tightly.

"I know you can do it."

There was something about his belief and encouragement that made her want to please him. Of course, his sensual threats also had her chomping at the bit to obey.

Yvonne was fiercely independent, so her desire—no, her *need*—to acquiesce to him in the bedroom, while surprising, was equally as exciting.

Of course, she revised her desire to please him when the bastard started moving again. Leo held nothing back as he slammed into her, taking her with all that force and passion that drove her absolutely insane. She loved being taken hard, and Leo was a master at it.

She pressed her face against his mattress, using that and the gag to try to shield any sound that might escape. Yvonne accepted that breathing would just have to wait.

Within moments, she was there. The nuclear bomb detonated, her body jerking roughly as every nerve ending exploded at the same time.

Leo came as well, his fingers tightening on her hips. She'd worn bruises there for a day or two after their last interlude and, like a lovelorn girl, she'd studied them in the mirror and run her fingers over them, recalling how it had felt to be with Leo, adoring them like he'd given her diamonds or pearls.

She had no idea if that was sane or not. She'd have to ask Sunnie tomorrow.

Leo had restricted her noise, but it occurred to her, he'd put that same limitation on himself as well. With the exception of one short burst of air as his climax struck, he was silent too.

Without the benefit of hearing his words or groans, she was forced to read his body language to fully understand how deep his pleasure ran.

He loosened his fingers on her hips, wrapping his arms around her upper body to pull her toward him. Then, in a standing spoon, he enveloped her, surrounding her, nuzzling the side of her neck with his nose and lips.

When he whispered her name, "Vonnie," in her ear, she heard the wonder, the awe, the happiness.

She heard it because she *felt* it.

He untied the knot holding his shirt in place and pulled it away.

Yvonne licked her lips as she turned to face him.

He met her halfway, kissing her as if he were going off to war, as if the plane was going down and they had seconds to live.

Then he cupped her cheeks, pulling back a few inches to look at her. "I love you, Vonnie."

Her chest tightened, her heart raced, and every single thing inside her sang. She'd never had a single sentence impact her so intensely.

"I love you too."

❦ 10 ❦

Leo parked his truck outside the pub, but made no move to get out. Instead, he lay his head against the rest and blew out a long, tired breath.

He hadn't seen Yvonne since the fair, since the night he'd told her he loved her.

He hadn't said those words to a woman since Denise. When he considered that, he realized they were two entirely different kinds of love.

With Denise, it had been that of first love, the yearnings of a young boy, who'd had his head turned by a pretty face and the fact she'd actually seen Clint Black and Vince Gill in concert. She'd been popular and fun and, to a farm boy who'd never seen much of the world, she was the epitome of cool. Looking back, what he thought was love, now seemed more like a simple attraction amplified by teenaged boy hormones.

He had *never* felt for Denise what he felt for Yvonne.

When he'd looked at Yvonne's face after pulling out that gag, gazed into those pretty eyes of hers and seen that twinkle of humor mixed with desire and need, he knew he'd never find another woman more perfect for him than her.

They'd snuck out of his bedroom after making love, peeking

into the boys' room as they passed. Both fellas had been sacked out, dead to the world after their long day at the farm and then the fair. The two of them hung out, cuddling on the couch, watching the rest of the movie until Ryder came home. Then he'd driven her back to the pub and kissed her good night.

And since then, the bottom had fallen out. Of fucking everything.

He'd been getting up at four so he could get to the farm by five to help his brother with the crops. Then, he drove his mom back into the city at nine, both of them visiting with his dad, who'd had some complications after his surgery. He left his mom at the hospital around ten, then headed to his house to grab the boys. Mercifully, Ryder had been able to switch his hours, starting later in the morning to help Leo out.

Summer break was almost over, and Leo felt guilty for feeling so much relief over that. Typically, he loved the summer months with the boys, but this year, it had felt like hard work.

And he was afraid his heavy feelings were obvious to Vince, who'd been stomping around like a bear with a thorn in his paw, scowling and quiet. The only time he spoke, it was with an irritated tone that went through Leo like nails on a chalkboard. He didn't abide rudeness, but Vince didn't seem to be capable of anything else these days, so they'd been butting heads nonstop.

To make matters worse, Vince grumbled constantly about having to go out to the farm to help out, which pissed Josh off, who took it upon himself to lecture his nephew about responsibility and the importance of family, which annoyed the fuck out of him. He'd tell Josh to lay off and then his brother would look at him like he was a shitty father.

His energy was nonexistent, and his temper had reached the boiling point.

He glanced at the back door to the kitchen of Sunday's Side. Yvonne would be there. That fact alone should have him leaping from the truck, but he hated showing up like this. Again.

He couldn't, for the life of him, figure out why she put up

with him. It seemed like all he did these days was bitch and moan. Try as he may, he couldn't find a bright side to any of this shit.

So much for her secrets to a happy life. He was the worst student on the planet.

His phone rang.

Leo frowned when he saw Ryder's name appear on the screen. It was Saturday, and Ryder was supposed to have the day off. If he told Leo he had to go in, Leo wasn't sure he'd be able to hold his shit together.

"Hello," he said, not bothering to temper the hostility in his voice.

"Hey, Leo. You still running deliveries?" Ryder asked, oblivious to Leo's anger.

"Yeah."

"Listen, the boys and I were just talking. Decided we wanted to go camping tonight. School starts next week, and I haven't had a chance to do any fun things with the guys this summer. Besides, I figured you could use a break from all of us." Ryder lowered his voice as he added, "Give you a night alone with Yvonne."

Ryder had been surprised to find Leo and Yvonne sitting very cozy on the couch together the other night. So much so, he'd been waiting up for Leo when he got back from dropping her off at the pub. It had been nice to talk to someone about her, and he'd been genuinely touched by Ryder's support. The two of them had been virtual strangers when they'd moved in together, bonded by sons who were brothers. Since then, Ryder had become a friend, even though there were times Leo got a sense Ryder kept him—and everyone else in the world—an arm's length away. He could only assume Denise's death had broken something in the other man, and now he struggled to get close to anyone.

"Anyway," Ryder continued, "we got the tent and sleeping bags out of storage. We're hitting a grocery store on the way out of town for campfire food, then heading to Point Lookout for the night. Told them we'd do some fishing in the morning, so we probably won't be back until mid-afternoon. You okay with that?"

Leo heard the words Ryder was saying, but they weren't fully soaking in. He was getting a night off. A chance to be alone with Yvonne.

Every miserable feeling he'd been suffering floated away. "Seriously, man?"

Ryder chuckled. "Yeah. Seriously. I told you the other night. I owe you."

"Thanks, Ryder."

They hung up and, just like that, Leo found his silver lining. That weight that never fully left his shoulders lifted and he felt free. He texted Josh to say he wasn't coming back to the farm as he'd originally planned, and that he wouldn't be able to make it at all tomorrow. His brother would be pissed as fuck, but that was just too bad. Leo hadn't had a day off in...years.

Marie was slated to visit their dad later and pick up their mom to take her home, as was their routine. So, the rest of the day was his.

And he knew exactly how he wanted to spend it.

He grabbed the crate of vegetables from the back of his truck, suddenly grateful he'd made this his last delivery of the day. Once he saw Yvonne, he knew he wasn't going to be able to let her out of his sight...at least until the boys got back home.

Leo walked through the screen door and immediately spotted Yvonne's cute ass as she bent over to pull a pie from the oven.

He wolf-whistled at Yvonne, not noticing her aunt Riley until the other woman laughed.

Leo turned and smiled at Riley. "You caught me."

Riley walked over and grasped his chin in her hand, turning his head this way and that, inspecting him. He was a grown-ass man, but the woman had a way of making him feel like a small child, and not in a way he hated. Her concern for him felt nice.

"I like the smile, but you've still got those damn dark circles under your eyes. You getting enough sleep?"

He shook his head. "No."

"Eating right?"

"Nope."

"Stressed to the max?"

He nodded. "Always."

"Dammit. That's what I thought. Yvonne, I thought we had a plan to fix all this?" Riley chastised her niece, who'd drifted over to them, amused by their interplay.

"He's a tough case, Riley. Rome wasn't built in a day."

"Speaking of building Rome," Leo said. "Any chance you can get the rest of the day off? I'm free until tomorrow afternoon."

The shock on Yvonne's face proved he really didn't take enough time off for himself. "I—" she started.

"She can," Riley answered. "You two get out of here. The next time I see you, Leo, I want you well-fed, well-rested and," she wiggled her eyebrows, "well-fu—"

"We're leaving!" Yvonne said, cutting her aunt off while Leo chuckled.

"You telling tales on us?" Leo asked her.

"I dare you to keep anything from Riley," Yvonne replied. "I swear to God, she reads minds."

Riley shrugged. "A clairvoyant never tells her secrets."

"Let me go grab my purse from the apartment," Yvonne said as they left the kitchen and headed for the stairs to her place.

They both waved at Padraig, who was leaning on the counter chatting with Emmy.

Leo placed his hand on her back and guided her toward her bedroom. "You might want to pack a bag. We're staying the night at my house."

"What about the boys?"

"Ryder took them camping."

Her eyes lit up. "You mean we're going to be *alone*-alone?"

He nodded, not bothering to temper the big-ass smile on his face. "Yep."

They entered her bedroom, and he sat on the edge of her bed as she grabbed an overnight bag from her closet and started tossing pajamas she wouldn't wear into it, as well as a change of clothing.

"Riley wasn't wrong. You look wrung out. Is your dad okay?"

Leo started to nod, then shrugged. "It's taking him some time to bounce back from the bypass surgery. I suspect some of that is due to the diabetes, but the doctor says he'll recover. It's just going to take a little longer than we'd expected."

"Will he be able to return to work?"

Leo shook his head. "Not to the same extent as before. He'll have to cut way back, and I'm sure he won't be able to do any heavy lifting for quite a while."

"Which I'm sure puts Josh in good spirits."

Leo laughed. She knew him and his family well enough to know his brother was a bear on good days. "His aggressiveness is no longer passive. It's outright pissed off. I want the farm to succeed and thrive as much as he does, but we have very different ideas about how that should happen."

"What does Marie say?"

"You know Marie. She's ever the peacemaker. Never takes a side, just tells us both we make valid points." His shoulders started to tighten again. Talking about his family never failed to stress him out. "I don't want to think about that today. It's my day off."

Yvonne walked over and cupped his cheek. "I love that you're taking a day off. And I'm stealing all the credit. I've had an amazing impact on you. Truly stellar results. Really, when you think about it, you owe me everyth—"

Leo reached up to grab her, tossing her to the bed and tickling her. "Are you seriously going to steal all the credit?"

She nodded unrepentantly. "Absolutely."

He stopped tickling her, dropping to his elbows over her, kissing the tip of her nose. "Good. You should. You're good for my soul, Vonnie."

"Just your soul?" she teased, reaching down to run her hand along his suddenly emerging erection.

"You're very good for that part of me too." He glanced over his shoulder. He hadn't shut her bedroom door behind them. God only knew how many of her cousins were home at the minute. As tempting as it was to finish what she'd just started, Leo was tired of sneaking around. The next time he took her, they were going to be completely naked and, if he did things right, Yvonne would be screaming down the rafters.

"You have everything you need?" he asked, forcing himself to move away from her. He offered a hand to help her stand as well, grinning at her confusion. Yvonne had obviously thought they were going to start the party here.

"I need to grab some things from the bathroom."

"Okay."

"Are you in a hurry?" she asked, clearly not ready to give up their chance at sex.

"Nope. I'm not. We have twenty-four hours, Vonnie. A whole fucking day. I'm going to put that to good use. Going to strip you naked and worship every inch of your body."

She flushed, the pink in her cheeks drawing his attention to her adorable freckles. She was the picture of a fresh-faced, all-natural woman. There was nothing fake about Yvonne.

"I like the idea of being worshipped."

He chuckled. "I'm sure you do, but first..." He started to open the drawer to her nightstand, but she grabbed his wrist to stop him.

Mmmmhmmm. Just as he'd thought. "What's in here?"

"Girl stuff, nosy. You ready?"

He shook his head. "You're not finished packing."

She gave him a funny look. Until he shook off her grip and opened the drawer.

"Leo—" she started.

The drawer contained the typical stuff—lip balm, a sleep mask, lotion, a couple pens...and exactly what he was searching for. Her vibrator.

He pulled out the slick blue toy and turned it on high.

"Batteries are good," he mused.

"Of course they are. I'm not a heathen."

He turned it off and handed it to her. "Toss it in your bag."

She gave him a curious look but didn't argue. "Fine."

"Come on."

She grabbed her toothbrush and tossed it in the bag as well, then the two of them exited through the same door he'd entered, saying goodbye to Riley as they left.

He helped her into the truck, then cranked up Luke Combs on the radio, serenading her with "Beer Never Broke My Heart" as she laughed. They rode with the windows down, not a care in the world.

This was the life he longed for.

Sitting next to Yvonne with no more on his mind than which position to try first and what food to have delivered for dinner.

Bliss.

He carried her bag into his house, tossing it to the floor by the door before reaching for her to steal a kiss.

Yvonne stepped into his arms, wrapping hers around his neck, her tongue touching his. He could taste apples and cinnamon—from the pies she'd been baking? Yvonne had a sweet tooth, not that he'd ever complain. She was as delicious as the desserts she made.

They parted when Boomer continued jumping up on them, determined to steal his own affection from Yvonne.

"What should we do first?" she asked, kneeling down to pet the spoiled dog as he tried to lick her face, his tail wagging.

Leo had been working off a list since the day he'd learned to read, everything mapped out, planned.

"Whatever we feel like doing."

She laughed, rising slowly. "You may have taken my advice a little too much to heart."

"I'm letting the wind blow me where it will. Wasn't that your idea?"

"It was." Yvonne looked over her shoulder, down the hallway. "Any chance this wind is going to blow you to your bedroom?"

He considered that, then shook his head. "Not right away. No."

Her lower lip came out in a pout that had him bending forward to kiss her. She was cute when she didn't get her way.

"Is the wind blowing at all?" she said as their lips parted.

He chuckled. "It is. In fact, I think we're due for a gale. Any minute."

She brightened up. "Oh yeah?"

He grasped her hand, tugging on it when she started to head for the bedroom. He hadn't been kidding. That wasn't his destination. He pulled her into the living room.

"We're not watching TV, are we?"

Leo didn't reply. Instead, he sat down on the couch and pointed to her. "Take off your clothes. All of them."

"Here?" Yvonne glanced around the room. There were blinds on the windows and they were down. None of the neighbors could see in.

Leo placed his hands behind his head and leaned back against the couch, letting her know he was ready for a show.

Yvonne didn't have a shy bone in her. And she didn't have any of those annoying hang-ups a lot of women seemed to have about their bodies. She pulled her T-shirt over her head, her smile the perfect combination of sweet and sinful.

Leo unfastened his belt, then unbuttoned his jeans, the denim suddenly too constricting.

Yvonne watched him, reaching behind her back to unfasten her bra. It fell to the floor on top of her shirt, and he had to unzip his jeans in search of more relief. He'd been at half-mast since leaving her bedroom, but now...now, he was rock-hard and hurting. Something he'd have to figure out how to control because there was no way he was rushing through one second of this.

Yvonne unfastened her shorts, sliding them and her panties off together. She toed off her sandals when they reached her ankles and just like that, she was naked. His own private peep show.

"Cup your breasts. Hold them up," he commanded as he pulled his dick out of his pants, running his fist along it a couple of times.

She did as he asked, her gaze locked with his. He'd never met such a sensual woman, one whose desires matched his so perfectly.

Not that he'd really been with that many women in his life. And up until Yvonne, he'd been with all the wrong ones.

"Pinch your nipples, baby," he urged.

She recalled his previous request for pressure because she didn't waste time giving the tight nubs a little tease. She pinched them hard, her eyes drifting closed as she did so.

"Open your eyes, Vonnie. Don't stop looking at me."

Her eyelids lifted. She didn't meet his eyes again, her attention drawn to something lower. He stroked his cock harder, a drop of pre-cum shimmering on the tip.

She licked her lips. Jesus.

"Come here." He crooked a finger at her, then tossed a pillow on the floor at his feet. As she approached, he lifted his ass, pulling his jeans down to his ankles. Then he spread his knees apart, making room for her to kneel between them.

Yvonne reached for his dick, but he caught her wrist, holding her back for a moment. "No hands. Just your mouth."

"But—"

"No buts."

"Leo." Yvonne was obviously used to using her hands as well as her mouth, so she planned to kick up a fuss.

He wasn't interested in hearing it. "In fact..." he said. He reached back down to his pants and pulled his belt out with one quick flick. "Stand up and turn around."

She rose, not fighting as he bound her wrists behind her back with his belt.

"You like being tied up, don't you?"

She nodded. "I've never tried it before you, but there's something about the way it makes me feel. I can't describe it. It just makes me...hot."

"I feel the same way," he confessed.

Yvonne twisted, kneeling before him again. "I'm warning you right now," she said. "I'm not always going to make it so easy for you. One of these days, you're going to have to catch me if you want to tie me up."

Leo hadn't thought it was possible for his dick to grow any harder, but he could swear it just tripled in size. "Jesus. We're doing that tonight."

She laughed. "Thought we weren't making plans. Thought we were flying by the seat of our pants."

He didn't smile at her joke. He couldn't. "It's on the schedule. Tonight. I'm giving you a ten-second head start on hiding, then I'm coming after you. And when I catch you..." He let his words drift away, let her fill in the blanks. From the heated expression on her face, he was tempted to ask her how she saw that scene playing out. Knowing her, she was taking it down the same dirty path he was. Hell, there was a good chance her fantasy was even kinkier.

"Now," he said. "Suck me, baby."

She shifted until she could run her tongue along the length of his dick, licking him like an ice cream cone.

He sucked in as much air as he could through his nose, praying he had the strength to hold out for more than a minute or two. The image of Yvonne on her knees, her hands tied behind her back, the head of his cock sliding through her pink lips.

Leo closed his eyes. Maybe it would be easier to keep control if he didn't look.

That might have worked if Yvonne hadn't started sucking.

Fuck it. They had all night. Taking the edge off this way might help his staying power later.

He gripped the base of his dick with one hand, the other splaying in her soft hair, gripping it so that he could control her pace.

He pressed her lower, probably pushing himself in deeper than she would have taken him herself. She gagged for just a moment, resisting, before something in her relaxed and she took him to the back of her throat.

Leo groaned. "Jesus, baby."

His fingers tightened in her hair, and she gave herself over to him, letting him take her mouth. Yvonne knew all the right buttons to push, sucking on the head, teasing him with her teeth, her tongue exploring as much as she could.

One time, she shook his hand off, lifting her head. For a second, he was afraid he'd pushed her too hard. He should have known better.

She used her shoulders to press his legs farther apart, then ran her tongue over his balls, taking one in her mouth, applying just enough suction that he thought he'd died and gone to heaven.

"Vonnie...God, Vonnie."

Yvonne finished playing with his balls, rising until she could take him back in her mouth again.

This time, she took over, bobbing her head up and down with just the right amount of speed and suction.

Leo was a goner.

"Baby, I'm going to...I can't st—"

His balls constricted and then he was there, coming with a long, loud groan, her name on his lips. Yvonne slowed her pace but never stopped moving, swallowing down every drop of cum.

Leo's head fell back against the couch as every ounce of

tension he'd felt these past few months drained out of him. He was a boneless, anxiety-free, happy-as-a-bird-with-a-French-fry guy again. It felt like years since he'd felt this...free.

Yvonne wasn't the only wild spirit anymore.

Apparently, that gloriousness was contagious.

He lifted his head at the same time as her, then reached under her arms to lift her to his lap.

"Okay?" she asked, nuzzling her face against the side of his neck.

"Better than okay," he murmured, clearing his throat. He reached behind her back to tug the belt free.

Yvonne made good use of her freedom, wrapping her arms around his shoulders, placing soft kisses on his cheek, his jaw, his throat.

Leo grasped her breast, playing with it almost lazily as they cuddled on the couch. Neither of them was in a hurry. Time was a precious thing in his life these days. Stealing these few hours with her felt like a gift.

She shivered as he ran his fingertips lightly along her side, and he realized the more they cuddled and caressed, the more she squirmed on his lap.

He grinned. She was ready for more.

And so was he.

"Vonnie?"

"Yeah?"

"Run."

❧ 11 ❧

Yvonne stopped kissing his throat and lifted her face to his. "What?"

"Ten, nine, eight..."

That was all she had to hear as she recalled his plans for chasing her, capturing her. She'd promised to make him work for it.

She was off the couch in seconds, darting down the hallway. She was naked, so leaving the house wasn't an option. Not that she'd take it that far. Though the competitive part of her regretted the lack of hiding places in the house. She couldn't hide in smaller places, like the bathrooms or closets, because she refused to trap herself. Her escape depended on her being able to keep moving if he got too close.

She darted behind his bedroom door in panic when he loudly called out, "One!"

Her heart was racing and she had to fight to quiet her rapid breathing. It was silly to run from something she wanted so badly, but Yvonne loved a challenge and she loved to play.

The way Leo's eyes lit up when she told him she wouldn't always make it easy on him told her this was definitely a shared kink. She could just make out the slight red marks on her wrists left by his belt as she'd given him a blowjob. It wasn't the first time she'd ever gone down on a guy, but doing it without the use of her hands was an entirely new experience, forcing her to be creative.

His groans, the way he'd said her name, the way he'd gripped her hair told her she'd been successful. Pleasing him was starting to turn her on as much as all the things he did to her. Sex had never been this way with anyone else.

She held her breath when he appeared in the doorway. She could see him through the crack from her vantage point. If he looked in her direction, this game was over before it started.

Fortunately, Leo's attention was focused on the closet.

When he entered the room, he made a beeline for it, opening the door.

As he did so, she slowly slipped around the door, trying to covertly move back to the hallway. If she could make it to the living room—

Leo caught sight of her at the very last second, and she saw him start to run toward her.

She took off, racing down the hallway. She'd almost made it back to the living room when he grabbed her from behind, lifting her off her feet.

Yvonne struggled, still determined to win the game.

It was like a kitten wrestling a tiger. Leo's years of working on the farm had honed his muscles to lethal weapons. The guy was seriously fit, while she spent the majority of her days taste-testing her recipes at the pub. She was marshmallow to his steel.

Turning back to the bedroom, Leo carried her—despite her squirming—as if she was nothing more than a frisky newborn puppy. Once in his room, he walked straight to the bed and tossed her onto it.

She bounced on the mattress, using that momentum to come to her knees, intent on escaping from the opposite side of the bed. Leo was wise to that trick too. His large hand wrapped around her upper arm and, in seconds, she was on her back with him on top of her, holding her still with his body.

She tried to push at his shoulders, but he was immovable, and her efforts made it simpler for him to grip her wrists and tug them above her head. Caging them there with one hand, he pulled his belt free from the loops in his jeans again. He must have put it back on during his countdown, while she was hiding.

This time, he used it to bind her wrists together before looping the rest of the belt around a post on his headboard. She tried to break free, but the man knew his knots.

He paused for a moment. "You know you can say stop, right?"

Her eyes widened. "I'm not really fighting. Don't you dare stop."

Leo laughed. "I think this is what a safe word is for."

"We don't need a safe word. It's us."

He gave her a quick kiss. "You're right. This isn't a game. It's us."

Yvonne stopped trying to fight the bindings on her wrists. Especially when Leo moved lower, lifting her legs, tossing them over her shoulders and lowering his head.

"Holy shit," she breathed as he held her open with his thumbs and ran his tongue along her slit. "Leo."

He sucked her clit into his mouth hard enough that she saw stars. Then he shifted the slightest bit lower, fucking her with his tongue, slowly driving her out of her mind.

Yvonne's eyes slid closed as she let the magical sensations wash through her. Unlike lovers in her past, Leo didn't treat this as a payback. He went down on her like it was his job, licking, kissing and sucking her for ages.

"Fingers," she begged, when his playing continued long enough that she needed more stimulation.

He lifted his head. Then, the bastard got off the bed.

"Wait! I was close. I just need—"

"What's the rule on your orgasms?" he asked.

Yvonne narrowed her eyes. "Not this again. Dammit!"

Leo didn't stick around to listen to her diatribe. Instead, he turned and walked out of the room, leaving her tied to the bed.

This time, she did fight her bondage, pulling hard enough that she wondered if she could break his damn bed to get free. It would serve him right if she did.

When he returned, she blasted him. "What the fuck are you doing? Come back to bed."

That was when she saw her overnight bag in his hands.

"Oh."

He chuckled. "Did anyone ever tell you that you have a temper?"

She lifted one shoulder, unrepentant. "I was an only child. Spoiled as hell. All the treats and toys were mine."

"Mmmhmmm." She could tell from his tone he didn't consider that an exactly endearing quality.

"Sorry," she murmured.

Leo sat on the edge of the bed. "I need you to trust me in bed, Vonnie. Need you to know that I'm never going to leave you hanging...unless I'm punishing you for something."

"Punishing me? What the hell would you be punishing me for?"

He reached out and pinched her nipple. "For coming without me."

"You can hardly leave me hanging if I've already come."

Leo's eyes went skyward as if he was praying for patience. "I chose to be here," he muttered to himself.

She laughed. Until he pulled her vibrator from her bag.

"You're forgiven for leaving the room."

He pinched her other nipple, hard enough that she gasped from the sting. "I don't remember apologizing."

She winked as she nodded her head toward the vibrator. "It was inferred."

"That's it."

He placed the vibrator on the nightstand, and she started to complain, but Leo moved too quickly, flipping her to her stomach in one smooth motion. Damn, he was strong.

Lifting her hips, he smacked her ass half a dozen times.

With her hands tied, Yvonne couldn't lift her head from the pillow. But she could lift her hips, and as she started to anticipate his blows, she moved into them, loving the sting, the heat, the taboo submissiveness of it all.

"Dammit," Leo murmured, flipping her to her back once more. "You like that too much."

She wasn't going to deny it. Not that she needed to.

Leo stood to take off his clothes as she enjoyed the show. Then, he picked up the vibrator again and shifted to the same spot he'd occupied before leaving the room. He turned the toy on high, letting it vibrate in his hands a few seconds as he looked at her, letting her anticipate how good it was going to feel when he slid it inside her.

"Please," she whispered.

"That's right, Vonnie. Beg me. Beg me to give you your toy... your *treat*."

"Leo," she said, when he didn't move to give it to her. "God, please."

He pressed the tip of the vibrator against her clit, and she reared like she'd touched a hot stove.

"Fuck! Yes!"

He pulled it away, just as the first twinges of her climax appeared. He repeated the same thing, touching her clit, then pulling away seconds before she could grab that last ring, over and over.

She was near tears, desperate, in pain. "Leo," she said when he pulled away the last time. She got it. He could definitely punish her. All he asked for was her trust. Which he had. Completely. The man had proven in a very short time that he had the keys to the city as far as her pleasure was concerned. "I trust you."

He didn't say anything. Just smiled as he slid the vibrating toy inside, filling her clenching pussy.

"Yes," she hissed.

He thrust the toy in all the way, the rapid vibrations tormenting her. She held her breath, and when that failed, she bit the inside of her mouth to hold off her orgasm.

For several minutes, she held herself there, in that perfect limbo, her body shaking from the pleasure evoked from the toy and the pain of trying to stave off her orgasm.

When he pulled the vibrator out, she sighed with relief even as she instantly missed the toy.

Leo lifted her legs until her feet were flat on the mattress near her ass, then he pushed them apart, leaving her completely open.

She jerked when he touched the tip of the vibrator to her ass.

Her eyes flew to his. He didn't say anything, but she got a sense he was waiting for her to say yes or no.

Anal play was fairly uncharted territory for her. Nothing more than a lover's single finger had ever broached that part. The vibrator wasn't exactly thick, but it was definitely going to fill her more than she was used to.

Then Yvonne recalled the belt tying her to the bed. She loved everything Leo did to her.

She nodded, just once.

Leo slowly pressed the toy inside. The juices from her pussy had made the vibrator slick, so it slid in easily. It was still on high, still pulsing forcefully.

Once it was fully lodged, he shifted again, picking her legs up once more, returning them to his shoulders. He lined his cock up, pressing just the head of it in. "You're going to share your toys with me from now on."

With that, he thrust deep, taking her with one hard stroke.

Yvonne screamed, all hope of holding off gone. She came roughly, almost violently, as Leo continued to fuck her.

"Jesus, baby. That vibrator..."

It was killing her too. She never would have realized there was such a thing as too much pleasure before him.

Leo kept moving, kept taking her, even though every nerve ending tingled from her first orgasm. Yvonne began to fear a second one would kill her. Her body simply couldn't handle how fucking good he was making her feel. It was insane but true.

Leo pulled out briefly, flipping her to her stomach again. Lifting her ass, he thrust in from behind and, at the same time, he reached up with one hand to free her wrists.

"Put your hands flat on the headboard, Vonnie, and hold on."

That was the only warning she got, her hands hitting the headboard a mere second before he gripped her hips and took her with a force that made her bones rattle.

"Yes!" she screamed. In this position, it was as if she was being doubly penetrated, doubly taken. Every forward thrust shifted the vibrator deeper.

Her second orgasm hit her like a tornado, whipping her up in its powerful gale, twisting and turning her until she lost all bearings, all grip on reality.

It was several minutes before she realized Leo had come too. And another sixty seconds before it occurred to her he'd pulled the vibrator out and turned it off.

He was breathing loudly, still lodged inside, though his cock was softer now.

Her head dropped to the pillow and her legs gave out. She fell flat to the mattress. Leo followed her, twisting to her side, lying on his back.

She lifted her head and turned to look at him. His chest rose and fell rapidly, but he was facing her, smiling.

"Am I saying I love you too much?" he asked.

Yvonne shook her head. "Not possible."

"Keep thinking that word doesn't feel strong enough."

She smiled, surprised to feel the sting of happy tears in her eyes. She scooted over a few inches and put her arm around his waist, his shoulder pillowing her head.

Both of them were skirting the edge of sleep, exhaustion from their exertions setting in. It was early evening and they hadn't had dinner, but there was no way she could leave this bed until she'd had a short nap.

"Love you too," she whispered before she gave in to sleep.

12

The sun nearly blinded her when she opened her eyes the next day. She turned away from it. Her sudden shift must have roused Leo because he turned with her, spooning her.

He'd woken her up twice during the night to make love to her again. The second time, they'd gotten up to eat, but their midnight snack took a sexy turn when they started feeding each other, then ended with her on her back on the kitchen floor, Leo licking chocolate sauce and whipped cream off her breasts as he took her.

"Shower?" he murmured.

She nodded. They'd taken one after their kitchen interlude, but the idea of hot water on her stiff muscles sounded like bliss.

Last night had been one hell of a workout.

Leo rolled away and rose. It took her a couple minutes more to manage the same. By the time she joined him, Leo had already steamed up the mirror with the hot water from the shower, and he was standing beneath the jets.

She slipped in next to him, accepting the long, heated kiss he offered under the water. Then, they took turns washing each other's hair and bodies. Yvonne mewed when Leo ran the soft washcloth between her legs.

"Sore?" he asked.

She lifted one shoulder. She was, but she didn't care. Leo dropped the cloth on the floor of the shower, opting to use his hands instead. He pushed two fingers inside her, fucking her with them, curling them to stroke her G-spot.

"I want to watch you come. Right here. Right now."

There was no question he'd get his wish when he added a third finger and rubbed her clit with his thumb. His other hand rested on her ass, holding her in place.

Yvonne ran her fingers over his slick chest, then licked him, nipping at his nipples as he drove her up the mountain peak.

"Leo!" she cried, too close to stop.

"I'm right here, baby. Do it. Let me feel that tight pussy of yours clench around my fingers."

"God," she breathed, his words the final nail in her coffin. She came, clinging to his strong arms as she rode it out.

Once her orgasm waned, he kissed her again, this one gentle, sweet, loving.

Then he turned off the water and helped her out, drying her with a soft terry cloth towel.

She wrapped one around her body while he grabbed a second, covering himself from the waist down.

"Breakfast?" he asked.

She nodded. She'd worked up one hell of an appetite. "I'll make it." She walked to the kitchen, rifling through his refrigerator until she found enough ingredients to whip up a decent omelet.

Glancing at the clock, she realized she'd be better off calling this lunch. It was nearly one in the afternoon. Fortunately, today was her day off. After bailing on her family twice this week already, there was no way she could have left them hanging a third day. Not that Riley or Dad would have said no. They knew her well enough to see she was falling fast. Dad had pulled her aside yesterday morning to tell her that he thought Leo was a good man and he was happy for her.

Boomer pranced around her feet as she cooked, so she snuck him a piece of bacon.

They'd just sat down to the table to eat when Leo's phone rang. He walked to where he'd left it in the living room, then came back to the table, still talking.

From his tone, she knew it was Josh. Leo had a "Josh" tone that was unmistakable, a weird mix of exasperation and reassurance.

"I told you I wasn't coming this morning, Josh." A pause. "Why would you think I was joking?" Another pause. *"Don't.* Don't do that, Josh. You know I care about Dad's health and the family. I just—"

Yvonne hated the way Josh treated Leo.

Leo worked damn hard, but, unlike Josh, he had a son relying on him as well. Vince needed his father just as much, if not more, than that farm.

"No. Mom didn't call me this morning. What did the doctor say?"

Yvonne put her fork down, not bothering to hide her eavesdropping. Not that Leo appeared to care if she listened. He mouthed the word "rehabilitation" when she silently asked "what?"

She gave him a sympathetic look, but Leo glanced out the window, clearly unhappy with whatever Josh was saying.

"I told you, Josh, with school starting, now isn't a good time to—" Leo sighed, then gave up, letting his brother speak his peace for a few minutes more. "Listen, Josh. I need to get off here. I'll head over to the hospital later this afternoon. And I'll see you at the farm tomorrow morning."

Leo hung up and leaned back in his chair wearily. He'd looked so happy before the damn phone rang, but real life had returned with a vengeance.

"Rehabilitation?" she asked.

He nodded. "Yeah. They want to move him from the hospital

to a different facility. At least for a little while, few weeks, maybe more. Josh thinks I should move back to the farm."

Yvonne frowned. "But Vince would have to change schools."

"I'm not moving. He's been pestering me about it since the night of Dad's heart attack. I keep saying no, but you know Josh. Once he sets his mind to something, he's like a dog with a bone."

Leo rubbed his eyes, and she hated seeing him stressed out again.

She looked down at the towel around her and had an idea of how to distract him. Tugging the terry cloth loose, she pulled it away, letting it drop from her naked body.

It worked. Leo grinned. "You lost your towel," he pointed out.

She glanced at herself as if shocked. "Oh? Did I?" Then she gestured to the towel around his waist with a nod of her head. "Wish you'd lose yours."

"Didn't we do this last night?" he asked, even as he stood up long enough to pull the towel off and drop it to the floor.

"Do we have a 'no repeats' rule?"

Leo shook his head. "Nope. I intend to christen every room in this house with you a thousand times over."

She picked up her fork. "Eat your omelet. Then you can have your dessert."

Leo's dessert was served in the kitchen, but it ended on a blanket on the living room floor two hours later, the two of them still naked, lying on their backs.

Leo glanced at the clock. "Ryder and the boys will be back soon."

"All good things must come to an end," she said sadly.

"Yeah. And now that we're moving Dad to a different facility, I'm not sure when we'll be able to steal a day like this again."

She reached over and clasped his hand in hers. "I don't care if we're alone or surrounded by a million people, as long as we're together. Maybe I can start cooking dinner here for you and the boys once a week, when school starts up again. Give you a hand with them."

He lifted her hand and kissed it. "I'd like that." Leo's phone pinged, and he sighed. "I suspect that's Ryder telling me he's almost home."

He stood up and helped Yvonne rise, the two of them going back to his bedroom to dress. She'd just finished packing all her stuff into the overnight bag when they heard a car in the driveway.

They returned to the living room, dropping onto the couch as Clint burst through the front door.

"Leo!" he yelled. "I caught a fish! Oh! Vonnie." He came over and hugged her. "I caught a whopper, Vonnie!"

She grinned. "Did you keep it? Need me to fry it up for supper?"

Clint shook his head. "No. We let it go. I didn't want to kill it."

Yvonne ruffled Clint's blond hair. "Good for you."

Ryder and Vince entered, their arms laden with sleeping bags and duffels.

"You didn't help us unload the car, Clint," Vince grumbled.

"Hi, Yvonne," Ryder said. She liked Denise's husband, whom she'd gotten to know a bit better since his wife's death. He was a quiet, private man, but he never failed to greet her with a friendly smile.

"Hey," she said, then she glanced at Vince. "Hi, Vince."

Vince didn't spare her a glance. Instead, he appeared to study her overnight bag sitting on the floor.

Leo said his son had been a bear lately, and it appeared the camping trip hadn't improved his mood.

"Did you have a good time?" Leo asked his son.

Vince shot Leo a genuine look that could kill and didn't answer.

"We had a great time. Perfect weather, though the mosquitos were murder." Ryder lifted a bag of apples. "We stopped by your family's farm on the way home and grabbed some apples and corn on the cob. Thought we could take steaks out of the freezer and barbeque. You're welcome to join us, Yvonne."

"Thanks, Ryder. If you want, I could use those apples to make a pie."

Clint jumped up and down. "Yes!"

Ryder laughed at his son's excited reaction. "Yes what?"

"Yes, please! Apple pie!" Clint was practically dancing.

As one of the older Collins cousins, Yvonne had spent a fair amount of her childhood babysitting what she and Colm referred to as the baby cousins, Darcy and Oliver. The only other child she'd ever seen with the same level of limitless energy as Clint was Darcy. She also danced whenever she was happy, and the sweet girl was *always* happy.

"Wanna help Yvonne bake a pie, Vince?" Leo asked. Yvonne got a sense he was trying to find some way to cajole the boy out of his bad mood.

"No."

Leo's eyes narrowed. "Vince—" he started.

"I don't want to!" Vince shot back hotly.

"I think maybe you and I should have a little talk in your room. You're being very rude to Yvonne."

"I don't care!" Vince screamed. "It's your fault."

"My fault?" Leo asked.

"You ruin *everything*. All the time!" There were tears in Vince's eyes, put there by pure, unfettered anger.

Yvonne had never seen the boy like this. His face was red and his whole body was shaking with fury.

It was disturbing enough that Leo's previous annoyance faded, his tone one of concern when he said his son's name again. "Vince."

"You don't care about me. Don't love me. If you did..." Vince was struggling to breathe, every word he said laced with malice. "I don't want things to change, but you don't care! You don't give a shit about me!"

Yvonne gasped, certain this was the first time Vince had ever used an obscenity.

Leo looked completely lost. "Vince, you need to calm down."

Ryder glanced from Vince to Leo, and then to her, and she could see he was just as confused by Vince's behavior. "I don't understand," he said softly.

"I'm not going to calm down," Vince continued. "I hate you! I *hate* you! I wish Mom was still alive. She'd take care of me—and then I wouldn't need you!" And with that parting shot, Vince ran from the room, slamming his bedroom door behind him.

No one moved for several moments, all four of them stunned into silence until Clint sniffled. "Is Vince gonna get a whipping for cussing?"

Ryder bent down and hugged his son. "Why don't the two of us go on back to my room for a little while, Clint? We can get showers, wash away the campfire smell, then watch TV."

Clint nodded, but as he trudged down the hall, he looked like a deflated balloon.

Ryder looked at Vince. "I swear to you, he was fine when we were camping. Laughing, carrying on. I don't know what happened." Even as he spoke, Ryder slid a glance in her direction.

Ryder had come to the same conclusion Yvonne had. Vince had been fine...until he came home and found *her* there. So Leo's son *had* seen them kissing on the Ferris wheel. And he didn't like it.

That answered the question that had niggled in the back of Yvonne's mind since the day of the fair.

Vince didn't approve of Leo's relationship with her.

Neither she nor Leo spoke as Ryder and Clint left the living room. Leo stood motionless, obviously as shell-shocked as she felt.

"He saw us kissing at the fair," Yvonne said, breaking the silence.

Leo nodded slowly, staring down the hallway. He hadn't faced her yet.

Yvonne's chest tightened, and she fought to take a deep breath. She knew what she needed to do—and she couldn't do it if she fell apart.

"He doesn't approve."

"He's twelve," Leo said, his voice devoid of emotion. She wished he'd look at her. With his face turned away, she couldn't figure out what he was thinking, how he was feeling.

Not that it mattered.

"You warned me."

That caught his attention. He spun to face her, his eyes narrowed. "About what?"

"About the reasons we shouldn't have..." She swallowed heavily, her throat closing. She cleared it and forced the words out. "We should have kept the status quo. Remained just friends."

He shook his head. "No. Yvonne—"

"You know I'm right." She hated the way her words were starting to wobble.

"He's a kid."

"And you're the only thing he has. You're his father *and* his mother. He needs you. And he has to come first, Leo. He *has* to."

"I'll talk to him."

The tears she'd been fighting sprang to her eyes. She blinked them away. "No. No. He needs some time to calm down. He's upset. And scared. You can't push this on him."

"What are you saying, Yvonne?"

"I think...it would be best...if we just went back to being friends."

He scowled. "No. It wouldn't."

"Please," she said, her voice breaking. "Please. I'm trying to do the right thing."

"This isn't right," he argued.

She held up her hand to stop him. "I'm leaving one way or

the other. We have to go back to the friendship or...I don't know how we..."

"How we..." His jaw was clenched as he prompted her to finish her thought, his voice tight.

"Please don't make me say it."

He stepped toward her, but halted his forward movement when she shifted away. If he touched her now, she'd fall apart completely. "So you're offering me friendship or nothing."

She didn't respond for a moment, then she nodded. Her entire insides were trembling, while Leo's suffering seemed to take on the form of numbness. She wasn't sure which reaction was worse.

"I'm going to talk to him."

"I'm not going to change my mind," she reassured. "I have to..." She bent down to pick up her overnight bag and started for the front door.

"You don't have a car."

"I'll call an Uber."

He followed her, grabbing the keys to his truck. "No, you're not."

God. She wasn't sure she had it in her to hold it together the whole way back to the pub, but she knew Leo well enough to know he was going to drive her home.

Mercifully, he didn't continue the argument in the truck. Instead, they rode to the pub in silence, the trip a far cry from yesterday's, which had been silly, lighthearted, fun.

She held her breath the whole way.

When he pulled up to the door, he reached for her arm, stopping her before she could get out. "Change your mind."

His demand, so typically Leo, provoked a smile, a watery one, but a smile nonetheless. "No."

He released her arm, and she got out.

Before she could shut the passenger door, through gritted teeth, he said, "Friendship."

She nodded, the ability to speak beyond her, and turned away, rushing into the pub and praying no one stopped her.

Somehow, miraculously, she made it all the way to her bedroom without running into anyone. Once there, she closed the door, locked it, dropped down on her bed, and sobbed her heart out.

13

Leo walked into his house and dropped down on the couch without even yelling out to tell the guys he was home. He sat there and stared at the TV but couldn't summon enough energy to turn it on.

He'd driven Yvonne home three days earlier, and his life had been a complete shit show ever since.

After dropping her off, he'd gone to the hospital, where his father had been engaged in World War Three with his doctor, who insisted he wasn't well enough to go home. It had taken Leo and his mother the better part of two hours to convince Dad to go to the rehabilitation facility, promising him it wouldn't be for long.

The rest of that evening was spent moving his father, then he drove his mom back to the farm and stayed with her until nearly midnight. She'd been physically and emotionally wiped out, something Leo could relate to. So he'd sat with her in the kitchen and listened as she talked about all her fears, all the things stressing her out. It had occurred to Leo that he was definitely his mother's son.

Vince had been asleep when he got home.

The next day and this one had both started at four a.m. with phone calls from Josh, who was "just checking" that he was up and headed to the farm. One of their hired hands had quit—probably because of Josh's award-winning personality lately—so Leo had spent fifteen hours both days working with the crops, as well as taking care of some paperwork he'd fallen behind on since his dad's heart attack.

Yesterday, he'd gone to see his dad after work, but today, he'd called en route and his mom, hearing the exhaustion in his voice, had insisted he go home instead, promising that his dad was settled in for the evening and resting peacefully.

He had tried to talk to Vince yesterday, but his son was giving him the silent treatment, still seething with an anger Leo had never witnessed in the young boy. He'd been too tired to engage in battle, so he'd simply walked away.

Tonight...tonight he needed to clear the air. Leo couldn't go on like this. He was strung out and so fucking tired. Of everything.

He pushed himself up from the couch and headed toward Vince's room, dreading the coming confrontation. He passed Clint and Ryder, who were heating up some leftovers in the kitchen for dinner.

"Oh, hey, Leo. Didn't hear you come in. Man, you look wiped out." Leave it to Ryder to state the obvious.

"Yeah. Vince in his room?"

Ryder nodded. "Dinner will be ready in fifteen."

"Cool." Leo hadn't eaten much the past few days. He simply couldn't work up an appetite.

He continued down the hall until he reached Vince's room. He stood in the doorway, looking in. Vince was playing a video game, beating away at the controller like it had personally insulted him. From the way his son's shoulders stiffened, Leo knew his presence had been noticed.

He walked in and dropped down on the edge of Clint's bed, facing Vince. "Turn that off for a second."

Vince slid him a sideways glance, then paused the game. He

didn't speak, not bothering to offer him a hello or even a fuck off.

Leo had considered what he wanted to say on the drive here. In the end, he'd decided there was no point in sugarcoating it or hemming and hawing. "I just wanted to let you know," he started, "that Yvonne and I have broken things off. We're going to go back to just being friends."

Vince's expression, which had been nothing more than scowls since the day of the fair, morphed to one of pure confusion. "What?"

His question took Leo aback. "We're not going to keep dating. You said you didn't want things to change and, well, we get it. Vince, I know the last few months...hell, the last few *years* have been hard on you. They've been hard on all of us. Losing your mom like we did, well, there's just no replacing her. She was a very special woman, and she loved you more than anything. But I hope you know that I love you too, that I'd do *anything* for you. It's been a crappy summer for you, and I'm sorry, but I promise from now on—"

"You were dating Vonnie?" Vince interjected.

That wasn't exactly the response Leo was expecting after his heartfelt speech. He nodded. "You saw us kissing on the Ferris wheel."

Vince shook his head. "No I didn't."

"Oh. Well, you got so angry the other afternoon when you got home from camping, when she was here, I assumed—"

"She's here a lot."

Leo wasn't sure he'd say a lot, though now that he thought about it, before they'd changed the status quo on their relationship, she probably did drop by once or twice a month, and she was almost always bringing them food.

"So you didn't know I was seeing Yvonne?" Leo asked. Now *he* was confused. If Vince didn't know about their relationship, what was that violent outburst about?

"No."

"Why were you upset after getting off the Ferris wheel, then?"

Vince picked at his bedspread, and Leo got a sense the boy didn't want to tell him the real reason for his anger.

"Vince," Leo prodded.

Vince lifted one shoulder. "There's this girl I like at school, Delaney, and she said she liked me too. But I saw her when me and Clint were on the Ferris wheel. She was walking around with this other boy in our class, Valentino. They were holding hands."

Ah. Things were starting to clear up. It wasn't puberty making his son a bear. It was love's cruel sting.

"I see. But that doesn't really explain the other day when you got home from camping. Why were you so mad at me?"

The scowl returned, and it was obvious Vince was *still* angry. "Uncle Josh told me we're moving to the farm."

"He *what?*"

Vince's tone became heated again. "You said me and Clint could stay together, that we could live here. I don't wanna live on the farm! I'm not changing schools either. I'm gonna ask Ryder if I can stay here with *him* when you go."

Leo felt his own temper spark. Not at his son, but at his brother. Jesus. Josh had been a pain in the ass for weeks, but to go behind Leo's back and tell Vince...

No wonder the kid was freaking out.

"We're not moving," Leo said, once he'd taken a deep breath and calmed down. As soon as he left this room, he was calling his brother and setting the record straight once and for all, on a great many things.

"But Uncle Josh said—"

"I know what Uncle Josh said, and I know that's what he wants, but I already told him—and now I'm telling *you*—we aren't moving to the farm. I'm not taking you away from Clint or your school. I promised you that when I moved in here, and I stand by my word."

Everything in Vince changed. His tense shoulders relaxed, his face cleared and, for the first time in days, the boy smiled.

God. Leo was like his mother, but damned if his son wasn't even more like him. Leo was going to have to find a way to help his son deal with his stress better. Maybe Yvonne could share her secrets for a happy life with Vince too since—

Yvonne.

"So you really didn't know about me and Vonnie?" Leo asked.

Vince shook his head.

"Well, now you do. So...how would you feel if—"

"I *love* Vonnie!" Vince exclaimed loudly. "Can she come here and live with us? She makes real food and cookies and helps me clean my room. And she likes Fortnite, even though she's really bad at it."

It was obvious Vonnie's love of video games was what truly sealed the deal for his son. Leo laughed and laughed and laughed. He laughed so loudly, Ryder and Clint ventured from the kitchen to see what the ruckus was about.

Ryder smiled at him. "Everything good in here?"

Leo nodded, then considered Vince's request. "Yeah. We're getting there. Maybe you and Clint should come in for the rest of this discussion. There's something I want to run by you all."

Leo crossed over to sit next to Vince as Ryder and Clint took the spot he'd just vacated.

"What's up?" Ryder asked.

"Apparently my brother told Vince we were moving to the farm."

Ryder and Clint both looked shocked. And upset.

"You're moving?" Ryder asked, alarmed.

"You can't!" Clint looked as if he was prepared to chain himself to Vince to keep them in the house.

Leo didn't think Ryder and Clint knew about Josh's lie, and their reactions confirmed it. "No. Josh wants us to, but we're not. If fact, I'm going to suggest some changes for the way we run the farm that should actually allow me to do more of the work from home."

"That sounds great," Ryder said. "Now that I'm through the training phase of my job, I should be here more too." He looked at Clint and ruffled his son's hair affectionately.

"The other thing is," Leo said, for Clint's benefit, not Ryder's, "I've been seeing Yvonne."

Ryder glanced at Vince apprehensively. At least Leo and Yvonne hadn't been the *only* ones to misread his son's outburst.

"Seeing?" Clint asked.

"I'm dating her," Leo clarified. "She's my girlfriend."

Clint, in typical fashion, bounced on his bed excitedly. "You are?! I love Vonnie! She plays video games with us and brings me milk with a straw when my tummy hurts and has Spiderman Band-Aids in her purse."

Leo wasn't aware of the Band-Aids. She no doubt kept those on hand for the boys. He was amused by Vince's and Clint's lists of Yvonne's stellar attributes. He had about a million and twelve things to add to it as well.

Leo looked at Ryder. "I know neither one of us has really dated much since..."

Ryder winced slightly. He always did whenever anyone got too close to mentioning Denise's death. The other man nodded.

"The thing is, I'm in love with Yvonne, and I'm pretty damn sure she's it for me."

Ryder smiled. "She's definitely it for you."

"Yeah, well..." Leo ran his hand through his hair. "We have to figure out what that means for *us*." Leo gestured around the room at the four of them.

"That shouldn't be too hard. We've been planning the renovations to the house for months, and we've got the blueprints from the architect. All we have to do is stop dragging our feet and hire a contractor."

Leo grinned. "As luck would have it, Vonnie's uncles run their own construction business."

Ryder rolled his eyes. "I've discovered over the years there are very few needs that Yvonne and Darcy's family can't meet."

The two of them laughed, then Leo jumped up from the bed as something else occurred to him. He'd been so stressed out and upset, he'd lost track of the days. "What day is it?"

Ryder seemed surprised by Leo's abrupt question. "The nineteenth. Why?"

"Shi—nanigans," he said, just stopping himself from cursing in front of the boys. From the look on Vince's face, it was clear he hadn't fooled his son about what he'd truly intended to say. Which reminded him. He still needed to have a word with the kid about his own foul mouth, but that would have to wait.

"It's Vonnie's birthday. Her party's tonight." Leo glanced at his watch. "Right now, in fact."

Ryder stood up as well. "I'll go turn off the oven."

Leo smiled, slapping his roommate and friend on the shoulder. "The four of us have a party to crash."

Clint hopped up from the bed, jumping from one foot to the next. "A party!" he shouted, then he started doing that damn flossing dance. "Is there dancing?"

Ryder laughed, trying to do the same move and failing miserably. "You're pretty good at that."

Vince laughed, and Leo soaked up the sound. It had been too long.

"Everybody get ready. We'll leave in ten."

Leo and Ryder went to their own bedrooms, while the boys scurried around in search of their shoes.

Leo hopped in the shower, scrubbing off the day's worth of farm dirt in record time. Then he put on clean clothes and prayed Yvonne would be happy to see him. See *them*. He wanted Ryder and both boys with him so she'd see exactly what she was getting into, but more than that, so she'd see how much they all wanted her with them.

With any luck, his unusual family was about to get bigger. Yet another new normal.

He smiled as he considered her secrets to happiness. With her, he'd found the real Leo. A man who'd learned to laugh and dance more, who'd learned to embrace the chaos surrounding him rather than let it get him down, who'd searched for his dream and found it with her. Tonight, he was taking a risk.

He was reaching out and grabbing his happiness with both hands.

Because *she* was his happiness.

❦ 14 ❦

"And now, for your viewing pleasure," Uncle Sean said, talking into the mic on the small stage at Pat's Pub. "It's Darcy and the Dreamcatchers."

Her family had closed the place for the night to throw her one hell of a thirtieth birthday party. Sean, Riley and Darcy had gotten together and organized a variety show as part of the entertainment. So far, she'd been serenaded by Aunt Teagan and Uncle Sky, as well as Fergus's new girlfriend, Aubrey. Her cousin Oliver and his best friend, Gavin, had wowed her with a few magic tricks, Pop Pop had led them all in a rousing singalong of "Finnegan's Wake," and other family members had done silly acts to make her laugh.

God only knew what she was about to be subjected to, but she knew it was going to be funny when Darcy and her best friend, Brooklyn, took the stage with Finn and Miguel. Yvonne knew none of them could sing worth a damn, so she tried to mentally prepare herself when the music started.

The foursome had choreographed a whole lip-synching routine of Paul Simon's "You Can Call Me Al." Everyone in the pub erupted in laughter when Darcy pretended to sing—she knew every word—as Brooklyn, Finn and Miguel handled all the backup parts and pantomimed playing all the instruments. The whole performance was flawless and hilarious.

Or it might have been, if Yvonne had been in a partying mood.

Today was actually the first day she'd managed to not cry. Though she'd had a few wobbly moments.

Leo had texted a couple of times since she'd broken things off with him, but they'd been simple exchanges of information, mundane stuff about moving his dad to a rehabilitation facility and letting her know the restaurant's vegetable delivery would be a day late. She suspected he was trying to prove to her that he could do the "just friends" thing by keeping the lines of communication open. But each time he'd sent something, it set her heart to aching again.

Darcy had been her rock, constantly trying to bolster her, though her cousin had been shocked to hear that Vince didn't approve of Yvonne dating his dad. More than once, Darcy had shaken her head and said, "But Vince loves you," which—though a sweet sentiment—only broke Yvonne's heart all over again. Because the truth of it was, she cared for Vince very much as well, and to think he didn't like her hurt almost as much as losing Leo.

Yvonne painted on a smile and pushed out a few laughs at her cousin's performance. She didn't want Darcy to think she wasn't grateful for her efforts. Under normal circumstances, this would have been the best party of Yvonne's life.

Instead, her heart simply wasn't into it.

Yvonne reached up to adjust the tiara her dad had gifted her with at the beginning of the evening, proclaiming her the party princess tonight and his princess forever. She'd teased him for the cheesy sentiment, but when he hugged her and told her that —cheesy or not—it was the truth, she sniffled and told him she loved him.

She looked around the room and felt guilty. Here she was, surrounded by family and friends who wanted nothing more than to help her celebrate thirty years of a wonderful life, and somehow, in the midst of it, she was unbearably sad.

She tried to shrug off the feeling, tried to find a way to live in the moment.

For weeks, she'd been trying to teach Leo how to get through life by focusing on the positives, by finding the joy in small things.

She needed to practice what she preached.

"Darcy is hilarious," Kelli said, topping up both of their glasses from the pitcher of margaritas on the table. "I love this song."

Colm, who was sitting on Yvonne's other side, rolled his eyes. "You would. Do you think anyone's going to sing anything from this decade?"

"You could always get up there and belt out a tune for us," Kelli said, though Yvonne knew hell would freeze over before that happened. Colm did not sing.

"This isn't karaoke night. Besides," Colm said smugly, "I already did my act with Caitlyn." He glanced at Yvonne. "Thought it was pretty good myself."

Kelli snorted as if he was crazy, while Yvonne laughed. Colm and her oldest cousin, Caitlyn, were partners in their own law firm. They'd written and read—via beat poetry style—a silly piece entitled, "Now that you're thirty, it's time for a will."

"I loved it," Yvonne said. She really had.

"Stick to law, Colm. Shakespeare, you're not," Kelli joked as she pitched a pretzel across the table. It bounced off Colm's forehead.

"Real mature, Kell," Colm said, but before he could lob his own salty cannon back, Padraig, the other occupant of their table, raised his hands.

"I'm calling for a peace treaty right now. Don't make me send the two of you to separate corners."

Kelli had been Padraig's forever friend when they were all growing up. And while she adored Paddy, she merely tolerated his twin, Colm, the two of them constantly bickering over silly stuff. Yvonne didn't have a clue why they rubbed each other the wrong way, but it had been the status quo since they were all kids, so no one bothered to question it anymore.

"Watch the show," Padraig said, drawing their attention back to the stage just in time to see Finn and Miguel playing pretend horns, their movements so synchronized, Yvonne wondered how many times they'd practiced this. The idea that they'd gone to so much trouble touched her.

"This is terrific," she mused.

"They've been practicing for the better part of a week at my place," Padraig said. "Finn and Miguel must've watched the video with Paul Simon and Chevy Chase a million times. Honestly, if I never hear this song again, it'll be too soon. Which is a shame because I really like it."

Kelli gave Padraig a pat on the shoulder, feigning consolation. Padraig laughed, then glanced in Yvonne's direction. She'd been watching Darcy lip synch, but had forgotten to school her features.

"How are you holding up?" Padraig asked. His question had Colm and Kelli both looking at her as well.

She lived and worked at the pub with her family, which meant it would have been impossible to hide her broken heart from them. Especially since her eyes were perpetually red and puffy from crying. She'd only managed to look halfway decent for tonight's shindig because Darcy and Caitlyn had dragged her into the bathroom upstairs and covered up all evidence of her misery under six inches of concealer.

Yvonne shrugged. "I'm okay. It's not like I lost Leo completely. We're still going to be friends."

"Damn," Kelli muttered.

Yvonne was confused when Colm nodded at Kelli's curse and said, "This party is finally about to get interesting. Thought we were going to make it through one whole Collins event with no drama."

Before she could ask what that meant, a familiar voice murmured behind her, "We're not going to be friends, Vonnie."

She twisted in her seat, standing slowly when she spotted Leo standing right behind her. Ryder, Vince and Clint were with him as well.

"You came." She'd invited him to be her date, but after what had happened between them, she hadn't expected him to show. Then she said, "And you said we *could* be friends."

"I did, but I lied."

Yvonne waited for him to continue. There was no way Leo would show up, with his family in tow, to tell her he never wanted to see her again.

When he didn't respond quickly enough, she asked, "If we can't be friends, then why are you here, Leo?"

"I'm your date, remember?"

Yvonne's gaze slid to Vince, who was smiling widely at her.

She looked back at Leo. "You are?"

Leo rolled his eyes as if she'd somehow lost her mind. "Yep. For this birthday, and every one yet to come."

"But...I thought..." Yvonne looked between Leo and Vince, trying to figure out where she'd missed a step or twenty.

"Happy birthday, Vonnie." Leo reached into his pocket and pulled out a small, flat wrapped box.

She smiled, trying to wrap her head around what was going on. The words sounded promising, as did Vince's face, but after three days of trying to force her heart to let go, she was afraid to believe.

She tore the paper off, then opened the lid. "A key?"

Leo nodded and gestured to Ryder and the boys. "To our house. We want you to move in with us."

She looked at Vince. "All of you want that?"

Vince stepped close, throwing his arms around her. He was growing like a weed, only a few more inches to go and he'd be taller than her. "I didn't mean *you* when I said I didn't want things to change. I didn't even know you and Dad were dating. I love you, Vonnie."

Yvonne didn't bother to hold back her tears now. She hugged the boy back, then gave him a quick kiss on the forehead, grinning when he crinkled his nose at her show of affection. "I love you too, Vince."

"I'm sorry for what I said, for what you thought."

Yvonne cupped his cheek and smiled. "Forgotten. All of it."

Ryder placed his hand on Vince's shoulder. "Come on, guys. Let's give the two of them a minute to talk. I spotted a snack table in the corner." He looked at Yvonne. "We missed dinner."

"Riley stocked the table with enough food to feed an army."

Ryder, Clint and Vince glanced in the direction of the snacks hungrily.

Yvonne took the key from the box and cupped it in her fist. She was going to love cooking for four hungry guys. They'd lived on their own long enough that she figured they'd probably appreciate her efforts on their behalf for years to come.

"After we eat, can we ask Darcy to sing that song again?" Clint asked. "It was funny!"

Yvonne didn't have to look around to know that her entire family was watching them. The collective whole took nosiness to new levels. The room, which had been loud as hell a few minutes earlier, was now quieter, their voices lowered. No doubt everyone was struggling to hear what was being said without making it look like they were trying to eavesdrop.

Leo noticed as well. "Do you think we could slip away somewhere for a few minutes to talk?" he murmured.

She nodded, then glanced around at Colm, Padraig and Kelli. "We're going to head upstairs for a few. Don't cut the cake without me."

Kelli and Padraig laughed and promised, but Colm, who had a sweet tooth as big as New York, grumbled, "Don't take too long."

Kelli slapped him on the back of the head. "Jeez, Colm. It's her birthday and the guy she loves just showed up and—"

Colm rubbed the back of his head. "It's Riley's red velvet, Kell."

"Oh." Kelli looked back at Yvonne and Leo. "Yeah. Hurry."

Leo took her hand and the two of them walked up to the Collins Dorm. She started to lead him straight back to her bedroom, but he stopped her, dragging her to the couch instead. "You heard Colm and Kelli. We don't have that much time."

"I know, but—"

"We go to your bedroom and this party is over for you. We can't do that to your family. Besides, Vince is down there too."

Yvonne pouted, but sat down with Leo, the key to his house still clutched in her hand. "What happened with Vince?"

Leo gave her a guilty look. "We misread the whole damn thing. He never saw us kissing at the fair."

"But he looked so angry after we got off the Ferris wheel."

"He saw Delaney there."

"Love letter Delaney?" Yvonne asked.

Leo nodded. "She was walking around with another boy."

Yvonne gasped indignantly. "How could she do that? Vince is a great guy. What a little tramp!"

"Um, she's twelve."

Yvonne crossed her arms. "I don't care. How could she trample on that poor boy's heart? There's no way this other boy could be better than Vince."

Leo placed a kiss on her cheek. "The other boy's name is Valentino."

"Oh," Yvonne said, slowing her roll. "That *is* a pretty hot name."

Leo laughed. "I love your defense of my son. In fact, given your intense feelings about his current and future relationships, I nominate you to have the sex talk with him."

Yvonne shook her head. Then she punched him on the shoulder. "You still haven't done that yet?"

"I've been building up to it."

Yvonne rolled her eyes. "Sure you have. Anyway...even if he didn't see us at the fair, you saw his reaction when he found me at the house after his camping trip. He lost his shit, Leo."

"That was Josh's fault."

"Your brother?"

"Ryder and the boys stopped at the farm for apples and corn, remember?"

She nodded.

"Josh told Vince that he and I were moving to the farm."

Yvonne frowned. "You're moving to the farm?"

Leo shook his head. "No. We're not. I told you, Josh has been after me to move back ever since Dad had his heart attack. I've told him it's not a good time for that—"

"I don't think it'll ever be a good time for that."

Leo wrapped his arm around her shoulders and drew her closer. "I can't live there again. I love my family more than words can say, but there's no way we could all cohabitate under the same roof again. Josh and I would kill each other within a week."

"So why would he tell Vince that?"

Leo sighed. "It's Josh. He's relentless when he gets something into his head. He probably thought he'd force my hand by telling Vince. Or, who knows, the guy thinks the farm life is the greatest thing on Earth. He might've thought he'd tell Vince, and Vince would be so excited by the prospect, he'd beg me until I relented."

"If that's true, Josh doesn't know Vince very well."

"Yeah. I'm calling my brother in the morning and setting the record straight once and for all." Leo turned slightly and pulled her completely into his arms, hugging her tightly. "These past few days have been hell, Vonnie."

She sucked in a deep breath of his scent, soaking in the smell of his shampoo. Leo always smelled like Irish Spring and fresh air.

"For me too," she admitted.

"I'm sorry."

She lifted her head. "No. Nothing to be sorry for." She held up the key. "So…"

"I talked it over with the guys. You know Ryder and I have been planning to put that addition onto the house. We even have the plans drawn up. We're going to talk to your uncles about doing the work."

"I'm sure they'd be happy to do that."

"Of course, in the interest of full disclosure, I should tell you we're sort of slobs, none of us knows how to cook worth a damn, and wrestling is a way of life with those boys. How do you feel about living with four bachelors?"

"Sounds like absolute chaos," she mused.

"It is," he agreed. "It really is."

Yvonne looked around and recalled Pop Pop talking about him and Grandma Sunday raising seven kids in the apartment. He called it chaos, then he'd said he wouldn't trade those days for anything. She may have grown up an only child, but she was a Collins, which meant she was constantly surrounded by cousins. Hell, they were all adults now, and wrestling was *still* a way of life for some of her idiot male cousins. She'd had to dive to save a lamp just last week when Miguel and Finn decided to practice some karate moves in the living room.

"What do you think?" Leo asked. "If it's too soon or I'm moving too fast, just say so. We can keep dating and we'll figure out a way to—"

"I'm moving in with you."

"And you're okay with the package deal? I mean, moving in with me and Vince is one thing, but with Ryder and Clint as well…I know it's a lot to ask."

"I'm fine with it. Honest. I love your family, love the home you've made for those two boys. And I'm touched that the four of you want to include me in that."

"You know, it won't be forever. Vince will go off to college in six years and then…"

"Then, we'll buy our own house. Start our own family."

"I'm not waiting six years to make a baby with you, Vonnie."

Yvonne laughed, smiling through her tears. "Excellent point. I mean, I am practically ancient now that I've turned thirty."

"I want a little girl who looks just like you. Want to spoil her rotten."

She gave him a curious look. "Thought you weren't a fan of how spoiled I was."

"You turned out okay, I guess, despite it."

Yvonne tried to pinch him, but Leo shifted too fast, bending his head and kissing her. She'd spent too many days thinking she'd never feel his lips against hers again.

This was the greatest birthday ever.

His tongue stroked hers and his hands slipped beneath her shirt, cupping her breasts.

Yvonne parted her lips, their tongues touching as she shifted, straddling his lap. Leo let one hand drift to her ass, cupping it, pulling her more firmly against his crotch.

She could feel his erection through the denim. She nipped at his lower lip, hungry, ready.

One second she was mourning the fact she hadn't worn a skirt, and the next she was three feet away from Leo on the opposite end of the couch, panting, her head reeling from how quickly he'd pushed her away.

"Dammit." Leo stood up, wincing and trying to adjust his jeans. "Thought we'd be safe in the living room." He gave her an amused, though pained look. "Clearly I was wrong."

"You're going to make me go back downstairs, aren't you?"

He nodded. "Your family went to a lot of trouble to plan this party for you. I wouldn't ruin that for any of you."

"This isn't going to be easy."

"I feel your pain, Vonnie." He held out his hand and she let him pull her up. "After the party, Ryder can take the boys home, and you and I are going to a hotel."

She grinned. "We could always come back up here."

He shook his head. "Nope. Need you somewhere private. I have plans for you, Miss Collins. Plans that involve stripping you naked, tying you to a bed and making you scream. Over and over and over again."

Yvonne closed her eyes and let herself imagine it. Just for a second.

When she looked at him again, she noticed his grin was more grimace.

"Neither one of us is going to make it through this party if you keep painting those pretty pictures, Mr. Watson."

Leo pulled his phone out of his back pocket.

"What are you doing?" she asked.

"Setting a timer."

"For what?"

"Five minutes," he said. "When this thing goes off, we get dressed and go back downstairs."

"Wha—"

Before she could finish her question, Leo had pushed start on the timer. Then he flipped her over his shoulder in a fireman's hold and carried her back to his bedroom.

"Take off your pants," he demanded, his hands already working to free himself from his own jeans.

Yvonne didn't need to be told twice. The second she managed to step out of them, Leo was there, lifting her in his arms, turning her so that her back was pressed to her closed door and then...

Yvonne sighed in bliss, the sound quickly morphing to a moan when Leo thrust in with one hard, fast motion.

"God," she cried out, gripping his shoulders to hold on as he pistoned in and out of her. Leo's muscular arms and the door at her back were the only things holding her up. She recalled their first time together. It had been just like this.

Fast, rough, passionate, primal.

Perfect.

He'd given them five minutes, but she wasn't sure she would need that long. She was already there.

"Leo, I—"

"Me too, baby. I thought…I'd lost…you." His words were broken up by his forceful thrusting, but she could hear the anguish. He'd suffered as much as she had.

"Love you," she said. "I love you so much. I can't st—" Her words were cut off by the orgasm she didn't even try to hold back.

Not that Leo cared. Her climax set off his mere seconds later.

"Jesus. Vonnie. Yes!"

They remained there for a few seconds, both gasping. They were naked from the waist down, only shedding the necessary clothing. They'd come at each other like wild animals.

Her laughter when she considered that was breathless.

"Something funny?" he asked, as the timer on his phone went off.

She laughed harder. "I was just thinking we didn't even need the full five minutes."

Leo chuckled. "It was a long three days." He slipped out of her, one hand on her hip, holding her steady. He always took care of her, always made sure she was okay. Yvonne thought that might be one of the things she loved about him. His considerate care, his attention to her needs.

They pulled their pants back on, grinning at each other like lovesick fools.

"And here I thought the key was my present," she teased, slapping his ass as they left her bedroom.

Leo kissed her on the cheek. "If that counts as a present, every day is going to be your birthday."

"Hey, I just thought of something?"

Leo took her hand as they walked back downstairs to the pub. "What's that?"

Yvonne brightened up. "I'm a Leo. So really, everyday *could* be my birthday. We were totally meant to be."

He rolled his eyes. "I can think of a million reasons why we were meant to be, but sure...if that works for you, I'll take it. As long as you're *my* Leo."

EPILOGUE

"Hello?"

Yvonne peered around the open doorframe and found Pop Pop sitting in his favorite chair with Reba on his lap.

"You stole my baby," Yvonne said with a grin as she walked into her grandfather's room.

"I borrowed her," he corrected. "Thought I'd give you and Leo a chance to actually sit down to eat."

Reba was only two months old and she was already spoiled rotten, preferring to be held constantly. Probably because between her, Leo, Vince, Yvonne's parents, all her cousins, aunts, uncles and Pop Pop, the wee baby hadn't spent more than a few hours without someone's loving, adoring arms wrapped around her.

"What are you two doing in here?" Yvonne asked.

"I was just telling my sweet lass what her name means."

Yvonne laughed. "Already? Are you sure she understands?"

Pop Pop gave her a wink. "Well, now, lass, the meaning of names is a tradition with me, and since I'm not getting any younger, I like to take my opportunities when they present themselves."

Yvonne claimed the chair next to him. "You don't have to worry about that, Pop Pop. You're going to live forever."

"Ah, you sweet lass."

"So what does her name mean?" Yvonne asked. She and Leo hadn't made the name's meaning a deciding factor in their choice. In fact, they'd debated names, agreeing on nothing, right up until she had gone into labor and he'd driven her to the hospital.

Yvonne had been freaking out about their lack of name when "The Heart Won't Lie" came on the radio. She and Leo had both said in unison, "I love this song." It was an old one, a classic duet with Reba McEntire and Vince Gill.

Leo had looked at her, and she'd laughed. "Reba?" she'd asked, as he nodded.

And that was it. Three hours later, Reba was there. With them.

"It means 'captivating.'"

Yvonne smiled. "That's sort of perfect. She's been captivating us since the second she was born."

"She has indeed. Speaking of which, do me a favor, my sweet Vonnie. Grab that picture frame from the table and put it back in the right spot. My hands are full at the moment." As he spoke, Pop Pop smiled down at his great-granddaughter, looking at her with so much love, it took Yvonne's breath away.

She rose and went to the table, gasping when she saw what was in the frame. "Pop Pop!"

"I thought it was time I updated your picture. The previous one was of you in that cheerleader uniform with Sunnie at the police/firefighter charity basketball game. Your life has changed a great deal since then."

Yvonne ran her finger over the picture, smiling.

"Your mother snapped that one the day you brought Reba home from the hospital. The second I saw it, I knew it was the one I wanted for the frame."

Yvonne hadn't seen this picture before, but she was definitely going to ask Mom for a copy. In it, she, Leo, and Vince were sitting on the couch, Reba in Leo's arms. He was gazing at his new daughter in wonder while Vince sat next to Yvonne, the two of them looking at each other and laughing. She could recall joking about what an overprotective father Leo was going to be, with Vince remarking that he was grateful to have been a boy. Leo had simply ignored their teasing. Too captivated by Reba.

Yvonne put the picture back on the wall, studying all the photos that hung there, amazed to consider how much their family had grown in the last few years.

Pop Pop came and stood next to her. "So much love and happiness on that wall."

She nodded. There truly was. "When I first started dating Leo, I told him I was going to teach him how to live life like a Collins, was going to give him advice that would show him how to be happy."

Pop Pop directed her attention to her family's photograph again. "I'd say you were successful."

Yvonne shrugged. "I don't know. A wise man once told me friendship was just as important as love. Sometimes I wonder..." she teased.

Pop Pop narrowed his eyes. "You're a minx."

"You were right, Pop Pop. The friendship Leo and I shared all those years has given us a strong foundation for the love. It's made everything between us perfect."

"Friends to lovers truly is magic."

Reba made a quiet sound, drawing their attention once more.

"I could look at her for hours," Yvonne confessed, neither of them taking their eyes from the beautiful baby.

"Another gift from God," Pop Pop said at last, looking at Yvonne.

She kissed her beloved grandfather on the cheek, the two of them returning to the chairs, sitting together.

"Captivating," she murmured, as she looked from Reba to her dear Pop Pop.

. . .

BE sure to grab Finn's story! Wild Side is out now...and it's a menage! You know you want it!

HAVE you read the entire Wilder Irish series? All the books are standalone, so they can be read in any order. Be sure to check out all of them!
Wild Passion
Wild Desire
Wild Devotion
Wild at Heart
Wild Temptation
Wild Kisses
Wild Fire
Wild Spirit
Wild Side
Wild Night
Wild Embrace
Wild Dreams
Wild Chance

FANS OF WILD Irish AND Facebook! There's a group for you. Come join the Wild Irish Facebook group for sneak peaks, cover reveals, contests and more! Join now.

BE sure to join my newsletter for a FREE Wilder Irish short story.

WILD SIDE

Finn balled up a piece of paper and lobbed it across the room, raising his hands and proclaiming, "Two points!" as he hit the trash can.

Fergus looked up from his computer and rolled his eyes. "Thought you were going to work on payroll today."

Finn glanced outside the window and sighed. The sun was shining, but not hotly, as the humidity of summer had finally burned off. The sky was so bright and blue and cloudless, it made it impossible for him to sit inside. September had arrived and brought cooler weather that had him longing for nights by a fire pit, candy corn mixed with peanuts, and hot apple cider with caramel vodka. Fall was his favorite season.

"It's too nice a day to be trapped inside."

"You're hardly tied to the chair, Finn. You can go outside whenever you want."

"The problem with that is, you're going to expect me to come back inside eventually."

Fergus chuckled and started typing on his laptop again. Business at Collins Security had picked up in the past couple of months, thanks to Fergus. He'd served as Aubrey Summers's bodyguard on her last tour, saving her life from a dangerous stalker. His cousin had impressed the powers-that-be at a large local concert venue, and they'd just landed a huge contract that placed Collins Security in charge of all their event security. As such, they'd been busting their asses the past few weeks, hiring and training staff, doing detailed analysis of the layout of the concert hall, searching for weaknesses in security.

Finn was thrilled that their business venture was turning out to be so successful. Before Fergus had returned from two stints in the Army, Finn had been wandering around somewhat aimlessly, clueless. He'd been pursuing a business degree, but he'd had no idea what he wanted to do with it. When Fergus suggested they go into business together, it had seemed like the answer to a prayer, and he loved basically being his own boss.

What he didn't like was pulling six twelve-hour days a week. Or working inside on a beautiful fall day.

He looked outside once more and sighed.

Fergus didn't glance up, though he clearly heard him. "Go across the street and get a cup of coffee. Take a break for a little while."

Finn stood up and stretched. It was a good suggestion. Maybe he'd even take a stroll around the block a couple of times to soak up some vitamin D. "You want anything?"

Fergus shook his head and lifted his water bottle. "I'm good."

Finn walked down the two flights of stairs, stopping briefly to say hello to a couple of women who worked in the real estate office on the floor beneath them, before stepping out onto the sidewalk.

They'd set up shop on the third floor of a business office near the waterfront. Fergus had liked the location, given its close proximity to downtown. Finn had liked that they were walking distance from his apartment above Pat's Pub and the fact his favorite coffee shop was right across the street.

The bell above the door tinkled when Finn walked in, sucking in a long, deep breath of fresh-brewed coffee and pastries. Daily Grind had the best coffee in the city, and they made the most delicious scones he'd ever eaten, though he'd never tell his mother that.

Mom, along with his cousin Yvonne, was the chef at Pat's Pub, the restaurant/bar his family had owned and operated for decades. Riley insisted that her scones were the best in the city, and Finn had enough sense not to contradict her.

Even though she was wrong.

He glanced at the handwritten specials to see what today's featured coffee blend was. It was mid-morning and he was the only one in the place. The rush was over as everyone had already grabbed their early-morning jolt and headed on to work. The place would crowd up again at lunchtime because the coffee shop also sold wonderful sandwiches and wraps.

A woman walked out from the back, wiping her hands with a towel and smiling. "I'm sorry to keep you wait—Finn Young?"

Finn looked at the woman, his eyes widening when recognition dawned. "LJ?"

Layla Jean Moretti stepped around the counter as he lifted his arms, the two of them hugging. "Oh my God. No one has called me LJ since elementary school. I'm just Layla now. I haven't seen you since..."

"Since we were eleven," he finished for her. Layla had grown up since then—and he was blown away by how beautiful she was. Tall and lithe, with porcelain skin and chocolate-brown eyes, she took his breath away.

She'd always been the prettiest girl in their class, with her long, wavy brown hair and dark eyes, but that hadn't really sparked his eleven-year-old boy interest. In elementary school, the only way Layla would have garnered his attention was if she'd been able to transform into a Pokémon.

"God, it's great to see you."

"How's your dad? Your brothers?" he asked. He and Layla had been classmates right up until the summer after sixth grade, when her mother died of cancer and her dad packed up Layla and her siblings and moved them to Philadelphia, where he had family who could help him raise his five kids.

"They're great. I mean, my brothers are still annoying-as-hell, overprotective bastards, but it's not like that's ever going to change."

Finn laughed. Layla, like him, came from a very large, loud, boisterous family. She was the youngest and only daughter, which meant she had four big brothers who had doted on her, while she'd given them a run for their money. "So what you're saying is, you're still spoiled rotten."

"Absolutely. As I should be."

"What are you doing here?" Finn asked.

"I moved back and bought myself a coffee shop."

"You bought this shop?"

She nodded. "Yep. The previous owner retired."

"I had no idea Mr. Shepley was selling the business."

"It wasn't really advertised. He and my papa remained really good friends even after we moved. He visited us in Philly a few months ago and mentioned that he was thinking about selling the store and retiring to Florida. How cliché is that?" she joked. "Anyway, he and I struck up a conversation and made a deal. He never even put it on the market. Mama had set up a trust fund for me and my brothers before she passed, and I decided to take the money and escape Philly and the boys."

Finn grinned. "Your brothers are great guys, LJ."

"Of course they are, when you deal with them singly. But when all four of them get together, it's hard work. I decided I needed a fresh start in a city where there weren't four Moretti brothers breathing down my neck."

"How long have you been back in Baltimore?"

"Four weeks. Spent the first two weeks finding and setting up my apartment, and the last two learning the ropes of the coffee business from Mr. Shepley."

Finn had been in the shop only twice in the past couple of weeks as he and Fergus had been working across town at the event venue, doing security checks. He hadn't seen her or Mr. Shepley on those visits.

"How many times have your brothers visited since you moved?" he asked.

Layla laughed. "Three times. They're insane. But I put the kibosh on their constant trips down here during the last visit. Told them the next time I was willing to see them was at Thanksgiving. Not that I expect that to stick." She walked back around the counter. "What are you doing right now? Working? Have time to catch up over a cup of coffee?"

Finn nodded, and then pointed across the street to his office building. "I've got some time. I work right over there. Third floor. Started a security firm with my cousin, Fergus."

"No way. That's so awesome. So what's your poison?" she asked, pointing to the menu.

"Coffee the way God intended. Black and strong with none of that fancy shit in it."

Layla clutched her chest. "A man after my own heart." She poured them both a cup of coffee. She added milk to hers, and then the two of them sat down at one of the tables.

"How's *your* family?" she asked.

"Same as yours. Still crazy."

"And your Pop Pop?"

"Still holding court at the pub, even though he's retired. My uncle Tris and cousin Padraig run the bar now, and my mom is cooking up a storm on Sunday's Side."

Layla blew the steam off her coffee. "I love hearing that your Pop Pop is still doing well. Your family was the best. I'm going to have to swing by the pub to see everyone. Landon still around?"

Layla had been a bit of a tomboy when they were growing up. How could she not be with so many brothers? So she'd raced around the playground with him and his best friend, Landon, at recess rather than hanging with the girls by the swing set talking about...whatever ten-year-old girls talked about.

"Oh my God, are you ready for this? Landon is marrying Sunnie."

"Your *sister*?" Layla grinned.

Finn shrugged. "They went viral a year ago."

"Viral?"

"Ever seen the video, 'Hot Cop Saves Sexy Nurse'?"

"Shut. Up." Layla shoved Finn's shoulder playfully. "That was them? I had no idea." She glanced around. "I'm going to have to look that up on YouTube as soon as I remember where I put my phone."

"I'm back from break," a male voice called from the back room.

Layla turned around and waved as one of her employees took his station behind the counter. "Great. Do you mind making another pot of decaf, Seth? I didn't have time."

"No problem." Seth started working as she turned back to him.

"It really is great to see you, Finn."

"Same." Finn glanced outside, reluctant to cut their reunion short. "What are you doing tonight?" he asked.

Layla shrugged. "Not much. Usually I just work here until close, then head home for a late dinner."

"Wanna go out with me? We can catch up over a late dinner or drinks at the pub."

"Okay," she said. "That would be fun. What time?"

"What time do you close?" he asked.

"Eight."

"Perfect. Want me to pick you up here or at your place?"

"How about my place at eight thirty? I'd love to change clothes first. Otherwise, I'll smell like coffee all night."

Finn grinned. "You say that like it's a bad thing. Here," he handed his phone over, "put your number in my contacts. I'll text you and you can send me your address."

Layla took his phone and added her number. He grinned when she listed her name as LJ. He was never going to get the hang of calling her Layla and it didn't look like she cared if he didn't.

The bell rang as a couple who looked like tourists walked in. Layla handed him his phone as she stood. "Guess I should get back to work."

"Me too. I'm sort of surprised Fergus hasn't already texted me to ask where the hell I am." As if he'd summoned the text, Finn's phone pinged. Glancing at the screen, he laughed, then turned the display to show her Fergus's text that simply said, "Coming back?"

She giggled, and then gave him another hug. Finn wrapped his arms around her and tried to ignore the way his body warmed as her breasts pressed against his chest, her soft hair tickled his cheek. Suddenly the smell of coffee was a pretty potent aphrodisiac.

Layla stepped away...and it occurred to him she'd felt something as well when he saw her blush, smiling at him shyly.

He let his hands fall away.

"See you later."

He nodded. "Later, LJ."

Damn. So much for taking a walk so he could refocus himself.

Now he was more distracted than ever.

Four hours later, Finn was staring unseeingly at the computer screen. He'd gotten fuck-all done as he played over his conversation with Layla, recalling how her whole face lit up when she laughed. The attraction he'd felt toward her was instant and powerful.

Ever since opening the business with Fergus, they'd been pulling long hours. Finn hadn't gone out on more than a handful of dates, always too tired at the end of the day. That wasn't going to be true tonight. With each passing hour, he felt more energized, excited.

He knew this technically wasn't a date, just two old friends going out to reminisce, reconnect.

So it was the height of foolishness for him to wonder what it would feel like to wrap those long strands of soft hair around his fingers, tugging it until her face lifted so he could lower his lips to hers and—

"Jesus Christ, man. Go home already," Fergus interrupted just before he got to the good part.

"Sorry."

"I thought the coffee would wake you up, but it looks like it did the opposite."

Finn told Fergus he'd run into an old friend from elementary school at the coffee shop, but Fergus had gotten a call before he could say who, so Finn had gone back to his desk and continued to fail at work.

"I think I'm going to call today a wash."

Fergus leaned back in his desk chair, and Finn noticed his cousin looked wiped out. "It's okay. We've been pulling some long hours. I think I'm going to knock off early too. Aubrey's coming home tonight, and I want to clean up the apartment."

Fergus had fallen head over heels in love with pop star Aubrey Summers when he was serving as her bodyguard. After saving her from a stalker, the two of them had found an apartment together nearby, which meant Fergus had moved out of the Collins Dorm—the name his mother had given the apartment he currently shared with his cousin Colm and his sister, Darcy.

When Aubrey's concert tour ended on the Fourth of July, she'd remained in Baltimore with Fergus, writing songs for her next album. She'd left late last week to do a few shows on the West Coast, and while she'd only been gone five days, Fergus acted as if they'd been apart for years.

"She's not going to give a shit if the apartment is clean as long as there are sheets on the bed," Finn joked.

"There's a good chance we won't make it to the bedroom."

Finn held up his hand to cut off the conversation. "Spare me the details of your well-laid life. It's been just me and my hand for too fucking long, dude."

Fergus laughed. "You need to find yourself a girl and succumb to the Collins curse."

"The curse has nothing to do with it. I just want sex."

Which was a lie. For a long time, that *was* what Finn wanted, to live footloose and fancy-free, to hang on to his single status for as long as he could before settling down and committing himself to one woman for the rest of his life.

But not anymore.

Their cousin Colm, the eternal bachelor in the Collins family, swore there was a curse hanging over all their heads that meant when they least expected or wanted it, love swept in, taking them all down hard and fast. Finn used to laugh at the concept, but as more and more of his family members went down— finding their true loves and moving out of the apartment—he was starting to believe there was some truth to what Colm considered dire warnings.

Yvonne had been the latest casualty. His cousin had recently fallen for Leo, a single dad, and she'd been spending every night at his place for weeks. He figured it was just a matter of time before she managed to move all her stuff over to Leo's. Finn didn't like to think about how quiet the apartment would be then.

Truthfully, lately Finn found himself wishing the curse would come for him. He was surrounded by couples in love, and damn if they didn't make it look pretty freaking awesome.

Unfortunately, with the business taking off, he barely had enough time to scratch his ass these days, thanks to the increased workload. So it wasn't like dating was on the table at the moment. Or, at least, that was what he told himself every night when he climbed into his empty bed, trying not to think about how lonely he was.

"Good luck with finding a hookup then. Though I have to tell you, you're missing out on something pretty awesome,"

Fergus said, shutting down his computer and stretching as he stood.

"Says the guy sleeping with Aubrey Summers, my teenage crush. I figure she was responsible for eighty percent of my wet dre—"

"Gonna stop you there," Fergus cut in. "After all, you're talking about my future wife."

"I knew her first," Finn grumbled.

Fergus laughed. "Being a member of her fan club in seventh grade doesn't count."

Finn grinned and turned off his computer, slipping his cell phone into his back pocket. The other benefit to this job was, on days when they didn't have meetings, he and Fergus adopted a casual dress code, which meant he wasn't forced to give up his blue jeans in favor of a suit and tie every day.

He and Fergus locked up the office and walked downstairs together. At the sidewalk, they went in opposite directions.

"Say hey to Miguel for me," Fergus said, by way of a goodbye. "I'll hop back in with you guys next week."

Finn waved, realizing his cousin would think he was going to see Miguel tonight. After all, the three of them had a standing Wednesday night meeting at the Collins Dorm. Miguel Garcia, a Baltimore cop and his best friend, and Fergus came to the dorm every Wednesday to teach Finn defensive tactics, as he hoped to start spending more time out in the field and less behind a desk at Collins Security. So far, he was pretty solidly terrible at everything they'd taught him, something that amused Fergus and Miguel way too much.

Fergus had canceled tonight to be with Aubrey, and now he was going to have to do the same.

He pulled out his cell and hit Miguel's number.

"What's up, bro?" Miguel said as he answered.

"Hey, listen, I'm going to have to bail on tonight."

"Oh yeah? Get a better offer?" Miguel asked.

Finn laughed. "Hell yeah. Ran into an old friend from

elementary school, LJ. We're going out tonight to catch up over drinks. Figure that beats sweating my ass off as you beat the shit out of me."

Miguel chuckled. "Dude. We've been at it for months. You should be kicking *my* ass by now."

Finn grimaced. He was no slouch in the muscles department and he was a pretty big guy, just like his dad and uncles. None of that was worth a damn compared to Miguel, who was built like a brick shit house. There wasn't an ounce of fat anywhere on the man. Probably because when he wasn't chasing down bad guys on the job, he was lifting weights at the gym or going on ten-mile runs just for the fun of it. Who the fuck did that?

"One of these days, I'm going to take you down," Finn declared. "So rain check on tonight?"

"Yeah. No problem. I might put in a few extra hours at the precinct. Been a couple of robberies downtown, local businesses hit. We can't catch the guy. Your dad put me in charge of the case today."

Miguel worked under Finn's dad, Aaron, on the police force. He knew Miguel was hoping to make sergeant when the next round of promotions came out, something Dad also knew. Clearly he was hoping to give Miguel a chance to prove himself and earn some brownie points.

"Nice," Finn said. "Closing a case like that would look good."

"I know. Have a good time with your old friend tonight. You guys drink one for me, okay?"

"You got it."

Finn hung up and continued walking to the pub, glancing out over the water, considering his conversation with Miguel. It was obvious his best friend thought LJ was a male. And he hadn't corrected the assumption.

Why hadn't he?

Finn pulled up short and walked over to the railing, staring off across the harbor. Well...he knew why, but it wasn't something he'd been able to successfully wrap his head around in any clear fashion.

Miguel was bisexual. Finn had known that since the first time they'd met, and truthfully, he didn't give two shits who Miguel slept with. That was his friend's business. His parents and godmother, Bubbles, had raised him with one simple motto: Live and let live.

Miguel was a great guy and one of the best friends Finn had ever had. They'd met when Miguel was partnered up with Landon on the police force two years earlier, and the two of them had really clicked. They had the same off-color sense of humor and irreverence for anything serious. They rooted for the same sports teams, listened to the same music, and were attracted to the same type of females. They connected on everything right down the line, and while Finn had lots of friends and close cousins, there was something that set Miguel apart from the others, that drew Finn in just a little bit closer.

He hadn't realized what it was until a few months ago. And when he did?

Fuck.

Finn had been struggling ever since.

He and Miguel had gone with a bunch of guys to Houston for Landon's bachelor party. In true stag night fashion, they'd all gotten a little—okay, a lot—shit-faced. Miguel had started flirting with Finn, which wasn't unusual. He was used to Miguel making jokes about his tight ass or Justin Timberlake hairstyle, and he'd always figured it was his best friend's way of trying to get a rise out of him. Just another way to tease him.

But that night, Miguel had let his guard down...and for just a moment, the flirting felt serious. Real.

There'd been a glancing touch, a look that revealed way too much.

Finn had panicked and played it off like he always did, pretending to think it was all a big joke, and Miguel had rebounded quickly, putting them back on the path of "just buds."

But Finn hadn't been able to forget that look, that touch.

Or the way they had made him feel.

"I'm straight," he mumbled, feeling like a jackass for talking to himself. He liked women. He *really* liked women. He always had. He'd never once glanced at a guy and felt an attraction. Never. Not once.

Until July.

Now, he wasn't sure *what* he felt.

He loved Miguel like a brother, so was that messing with his head? Was that making him think he was feeling an attraction when it was really just affection?

He pushed away from the railing and started for his apartment, doing the same thing he'd done for two months. He shoved away his confusion over Miguel and turned his thoughts to something simpler.

LJ. Layla.

He grinned as he thought about seeing her again, ignoring the tiny voice in the back of his head that said he should have told Miguel his old friend was a woman.

Wild Side is out now

ABOUT THE AUTHOR

Virginia native Mari Carr is a New York Times and USA TODAY bestseller of contemporary romance novels. With over two million copies of her books sold, Mari was the winner of the Romance Writers of America's Passionate Plume award for her novella, Erotic Research. She has over a hundred published works, including her popular Wild Irish and Compass books, along with the Trinity Masters series she writes with Lila Dubois.

Follow Mari:
www.maricarr.com
mari@maricarr.com

* 9 7 8 1 9 5 8 0 5 6 5 4 7 *